To Bette

all the best

to you and

your family

George

2004

Alicia Maravilla

PUBLISHED BY IVY HOUSE PUBLISHING GROUP
5122 Bur Oak Circle, Raleigh, NC 27612
United States of America
919-782-0281
www.ivyhousebooks.com

ISBN: 1-57197-348-6
Library of Congress Control Number: 2002113071

Printed in the United States of America

Alicia Maravilla

S. Lecomte

Ivy House
Publishing Group
www.ivyhousebooks.com

La vida es sueño
(Life is a dream)
~ Pedro Calderón de la Barca
(1600-1681)

This novel is dedicated to Denise Lassaw, who was the first person to appreciate Alicia Maravilla when she was Candida and I was Alicia Maravilla, who then became her author.

-1-

A Mother's Dream

The sun had gone down into the desert sand to burn the flesh of other men and women on the other side of the world. The moon was howling at the dogs below that roamed from porch to porch like the children and roaches in search of a better bite to eat, only to be disappointed by the sameness.

Alicia sat on her porch, waiting for the next thought to free her from the air she had breathed for seventeen years at the same rate. Her mother was slapping frijoles against tortillas and cursing God first, then the men, Mexican men in particular, with a lack of forgiveness that the village priest could hear all the way from his confessional.

Alicia and her mother had stopped going to church the day Rosario, her only living brother, had set fire to the church while lighting a candle for his dead father. Prayers turned to damnation as Rosario watched a thousand fiery tongues lap up Jesus and his saints, sending them to Hell for all eternity.

Everyone in the village now had a reference point in history: the day Rosario burned down the church. Rosario, who had up to that day believed in God and His host of angels, turned proud atheist when the people at first demanded that he burn with the church, especially the old toothless women who had been deprived of an avenue to Heaven.

Alicia Maravilla

The church was quickly rebuilt, but Alicia, who had at first cried and cursed Rosario, did not have her first communion. At the beginning it was burdensome because she had to carry unforgiven sins with her everywhere she went, until she realized that in time she wouldn't remember any of them. Even peccadilloes, such as God only knows, no longer bothered her because the priest was not there to define them. Although she felt she needed absolution for the sake of it, she was none the worse for lack of it.

The moon traveled to Juanita's hovel and howled above the roof. Her husband became the pale full moon and yelled in the valley. The drunken voice was echoed, and the moon spoke in gibberish, complaining that women were only good at getting pregnant, at stealing food and making men feel miserable or else they wouldn't be getting drunk every night. Faces were slapped. The moon bled from its nose as the men were appeased by the sacrifice made to them by violence. They slapped the women's breasts like children discontent with the milk that life had doled out. The moon cried cold tears, and the air became moist. The men's voices died in the cracks in the earth and were swallowed by the women's flesh. They sucked at the breasts to appease the devil in their bodies, and the moon traveled on to the next valley, the next world.

Father Romero's porcine face pierced through the dark, pale as a wax candle. His lips were always covered with grease from the chicken wings he sucked on as avidly as a snake, hungry for the flesh that cured him from perdition here on earth. Father Romero was chewing on another chicken wing as he stopped in front of Alicia and said his buenas noches without the admonitions that had stopped firing from his mouth the day his porkish ass was seen running naked through the dusty streets. That day was another reference point in history: the day Father Romero was caught with his pants down at Jacinto's house, in Jacinto's bed with Jacinto's wife.

2

For weeks Father Romero had hidden in the dark recesses of the church and listened to confessions that came only from those who were about to die. Then one day, even though this was soon to be the twenty-first century on other parts of this planet, Father Romero came out of the church naked as a pig without hair, his skin as white as snow that never hits the ground here, and began beating his private parts with the heads of cactus. Everyone in the village came to see Father Romero, including the men who normally do not come to church. The men, of course, thought the poor hombre had gone loco and blamed it all on his many hours of praying.

Jacinto had also shown up to see the only circus show he would ever see in his lifetime before being shot by a jealous husband in a neighboring village. Jacinto, seeing the priest naked and vulnerable, picked up a rock and threw it at the priest's testicles. He missed. The men laughed, while the women crossed themselves, ready to give Father Romero his last and only send-off to Purgatory. Not being one to take a joke lightly, Jacinto picked up a larger rock and was joined by Pepe, Miguel, and Ramón, the Maldonado brothers, in case he missed again. Seeing how he was outnumbered by a sober bunch, Father Romero began backing towards the church like a martyr who had suddenly had a change of heart and wanted off the cross so that he could enjoy life another day. That's how much he enjoyed chicken wings and Jacinto's wife, whose haunches he now enjoyed in the recesses of the confessional where forgiveness was automatic. And if sinning and forgiveness occurred simultaneously what good was the sin?

As Father Romero stood before Alicia, he licked his lips and said, "I'm only human, Alicia. A man has to have a little fun in life!"

Whenever he repeated these words, Alicia felt better and what sins she thought she might recall at the sight of his rotund body all vanished like doves in the distance. She stared at him until he stopped chewing his wings. He opened his mouth, and chickens cackled out of it, chased by the children he had sired so that he could have his own private choir. Rosario's birth was also suspect since her mother had admitted to all her girlfriends that she too had gone to Father Romero for a taste of the Holy Spirit.

"I'm only human, Alicia. I wanted a family of my own, but the church denied me that right. Now I have sons and daughters I can adore as I see them pass by me in the streets. Maybe you'll understand later."

"Nobody said you had to be a bull! I think you are a liar and a cheat!"

"We're all human!"

"It's so easy for you to say! There are sins you should account for!"

"Not the ones that make us love."

"Rosario doesn't love you."

"I know he likes to think that Roberto Maldonado was his father. That's okay. Don't kill yourself with pride, Alicia!"

Father Romero's body was swallowed by the darkness ahead where he danced with women in the night, his naked flesh slapping his penis and testicles in a frenzy against the buttocks of a prostitute or newly born virgin, seeking forgiveness and flagellation in the name of humanity instead of the God he had abandoned but preached to the people who needed Him still. The moon seemed to smile as Alicia saw it slide above the church.

Rosario's skeletal body emerged with a plate of tortillas and frijoles, his eyes jealous as a coyote's. He handed her the plate and cursed her because she was not like his mother. Alicia had not spent as much time in the kitchen as Rosario had. As he cursed her, the air became cool, and his testicles and penis fell off. His face was relieved of the burden he had had to carry. Without these male parts he could be as idle as

Alicia and listen to English language tapes instead of washing dishes. Rosario resented the role his mother had imposed on him. He would become just another male doomed to reproduction, and drinking, and he would perhaps die by the gun. Only in Alicia could her mother set her hopes.

A stray mutt carried off Rosario's penis and testicles and chewed on the meat that was as rare as the fish that once swam abundantly in the river below. Rosario smiled as he pointed to his vagina and small breasts.

"Now that I am a girl, I can sit here and do nothing like the rest of you women!"

Alicia took the plate from him and began eating. Rosario stood in front of her like a beggar waiting for a response. She called him a stupid boy through the frijoles in her mouth and shooed him away as if he were a fly. He flapped his black wings several times and farted right in her face, still waiting for a response that would give him a reason to move. There was a time when he worshiped her like a goddess because she had allowed him to suck on her breast for comfort when there had been little food.

Rosario grabbed his penis and testicles from the dog and yelled at Alicia.

"I'm a man! Why should I become a woman? Women are stupid, and I'll never be stupid! I'm going to get a gun and kill the man who killed my father!"

"Father Romero is your father, Rosario. Get that through your stubborn skull!"

Hearing those words, Rosario came alive and ran off into the dark desert like Jesus Christ, in search of his real father. As he did every night, Rosario perched himself over his father's cross like a small innocent vulture doomed to soar above the abyss without knowledge of his own origins. The man he called his father was named Jesús, not to be confused with the real man after whom he had been named. This man, still not to be confused with the Son of God and the Holy Ghost, slept with Rosario's mother for a year until he was shot by a stray bullet during a bank holdup while he had been waiting to make a withdrawal. After the incident, many of the men believed he had gone into the bank to rob it as he had often wished to do. Rosario now believed that the man Jesús was not only his father but a well-known bandito after whom songs were still sung to inspire young men to heroic deeds. Rosario thought he would like to have a song sung after him.

Rosario sat by his father's skeletal figure and called him "Papá" until tears drowned his soul with the knowledge that he too was the seed of someone known.

"Papá, I will avenge your death when I am bigger. And your honor! I will kill the stupid priest for dishonoring my mother, your wife. And I will rob a thousand banks and give the money to the poor. And I will never marry. I hate women, Papá!"

His skeletal father did not respond and allowed him to believe that he was a true hero because songs are truer to life than life itself.

Rosario's small black vulture wings flapped wildly past Alicia and disappeared into the house where his mother yelled at the man-to-be for crashing against the table and spilling what food there was on it. Alicia would have gone inside to help, but she had her orders to sit and study English as she had for the past twelve years.

Alicia opened her book and turned the cassette player on: Lesson one hundred and fifty—Eating in an American Restaurant in New York. A man and woman are seated in an expensive restaurant speaking about the menu.

"Do you want to order asparagus today, dear?" the woman asked. Her voice seemed as friendly as a rattlesnake waiting in ambush because Alicia couldn't understand the word 'asparagus.' She knew it was edible, but what was the use of a word without a picture? Luckily her mother had scraped pesos for years for her to have a pictorial dictionary where she turned to the word and picture. The word was still strange to her, especially with the picture that reminded her of Rosario's penis going to seed at the head. The vegetable was disgusting, she thought, and she would never eat it if offered in any restaurant.

The man on the tape seemed to be of Alicia's opinion as he refused the asparagus outright and ordered spinach instead. Alicia had tasted spinach twice and had not liked it in spite of being hungry.

"¡Aunque tenga hambre, no voy a comer mierda!" Alicia would say even as a small child and would receive a, perhaps not well-deserved, slap on the cheek for using words that should not have been used by a young lady about to order asparagus, baked potato, sour cream, succulent roast beef and a bottle of red wine. The translation of her phrase would have set any Baptist's ears on fire, but since there were no Baptists where she lived, the phrase remained unharmed and uncensored. Besides, why should it be translated when the phrase was true? Even though she was hungry, she wasn't about to eat shit!

Her mother had told her that American women were ladies and not sluts. Apparently her mother was stuck in the movies of the forties and fifties and had not kept up with the changes in the United States for lack of a decent movie theater and a television set that some of her neighbors had starved to have on credit. Even though she could have gone next door to Violeta's to watch the soaps and commercials, her mother became religiously anti-technology and refused to have her daughter exposed to candy, cigarettes, beer, sex, hemorrhoids, violence, rape, and bombings, all of which she could see without a television set right outside her window. America to her mother was the land of pure snow, of polite men who opened

7

doors for the women and who lit their cigarettes, who kissed your hand, then your lips with the gentleness of a morning breeze. These men made in the U.S.A. were all like wonderful dolls in tuxedos. They never yelled. They spoke to their women.

Alicia couldn't believe that her mother could be so blind when messages from the north contradicted her fantasies. Everyone in the village was aware of her mother's dream and thought she was out of her mind. They told her so, but she wouldn't believe them. It was they who were crazy for staying in a hole in the ground like prairie dogs who come out to look at the sun, take a piss, eat some seeds and run back into the hole.

They accused her of being blind, crazy, stupid, cruel, disloyal to her own country for loving images of a place not her own. They too had sent relatives north with dreams of their own that were shattered because they were not their own. María's nephew had crossed the river like a desert rat, only to be shot by a border patrol. Father Romero's youngest brother married an Anglo woman at the University of Missouri and was killed by a runaway bus.

"Even busses don't like our kind. And where the hell is Missouri?" someone had repeated over the years, and the phrase had become a sort of banner. "Where the hell is Missouri?" someone would say when another expressed a dream beyond his or her reach. The poor dreamer would shake his head and wake up from his torpor, and he or she would admit, "Where the hell is Missouri?" It was too far for most whose feet were stuck in the clay of their origins, but still, a few made it across. Many were returned by bus, only to jump back into the river and swim across to see what they could find.

One day a letter came to the widow's house. Although she wasn't the only widow in the village, she was the only one who had been married seven times in a period of ten years and lost every husband she had to bullets from jealous men who thought she belonged to them. She had given birth to sixteen sons in spite of having been married only ten years. Everyone felt sorry for her because she had no daughters. Many of her sons were rotting in jail for stealing from tourists who had to find something scenic to photograph before they went home. Two of her sons were shot while trafficking cocaine. One of her sons, Trujillo, made it across and had not been heard from in seven years.

One day a letter came to the widow's house. It was from Trujillo. As soon as the letter arrived, the news traveled from house to house like a brush fire, and everyone rushed to the widow's house. Everyone first thought that Trujillo had committed some terrible crime and that he was going to be fried on the electric chair like a tortilla burned beyond recognition. The widow came out and relieved everyone of their fear by waving a check for ten thousand dollars and a letter from Trujillo himself. He was now the president of his own company—a fleet of trucks that delivered tomatoes all over the United States. Everyone, except for a few jealous faces, was glad for the widow. There was hope after all. A month later, after Alicia's departure, it came out that Trujillo was only a janitor, but a rich one.

Alicia's mother felt vindicated by the news and was more convinced than anyone that the U.S. was the land of milk and honey. Alicia, however, wasn't so sure, but the lessons she was taking put images into her head, and after listening to the man and woman ordering from a New York menu, she washed down the asparagus, roast beef and cream cheese topped with strawberries with red wine. Alicia licked her lips and wondered why she had to eat frijoles all her life until she got fat like the rest of the village women.

Alicia, according to her mother and the boys, now young men, who had courted her, was as pretty as the Immaculate Conception. Others, with better eyes and less fantastic minds, thought she looked like a movie star but that she would make a fine mother to their children. José had offered her his pet frog to have a peek at her vagina. Miguel had offered her his mother's shawl and three hundred pesos to touch her breast. Many had offered themselves. Some said they would change the face of the earth for her and were now in jail dreaming of her.

José, the man, now stood before her as she was eating more asparagus so that she would know what a lady felt like. Just as she was about to cut the roast beef, she noticed him from the corner of her eye but didn't acknowledge his presence.

"Alicia," he whispered so as not to raise her mother's wrath.

Alicia continued to eat her roast beef.

"Please, Alicia. I love you. Won't you take pity on me? My heart is aching for you. You have mistreated me ever since I was a young boy, but I love you. Don't go north, my lovely one. There's nothing but snakes and vultures. And the Anglos all have cold hearts! They don't care for their women. Haven't you ever seen their blue eyes, Alicia? You must marry one of your own!"

Hearing José's nonsense, Alicia dropped the glass of wine, tore the earphones from her head and began yelling at José as if he symbolized all the Mexican men.

"I am not your woman or wife just because you want me! I am not your woman just because you pray to have me. And God cannot make me love you or anyone else! I will marry who I want, José! You men are all alike here. All you will do is beat me and make me cry and have sons like yourselves. I don't want to have any children, José. Could you live with that?"

10

"Women are meant to have children, Alicia. Read your Bible!"

"I don't need the Bible to tell me what to do, José. Especially when I should or shouldn't have children!"

"Why don't you act like a woman, instead of a man?"

"You see!"

"See what?"

"Don't you men ever hear yourselves? You are putting me down already, and I am not even your wife. You want an obedient wife who will have a belly full of children. Marry a fish, José, they have many babies all at once."

"You're nothing but a puta! I still remember the frog! You can be bought for a frog!"

"You're nothing but a pendejo, José! My tía María's sow wouldn't have you for a husband!"

The front door slammed open, and Alicia's mother, once the flower of the village, now a short woman with swollen flesh, emerged like a witch out of a fairy tale and began yelling at José for standing too close to her daughter, even if he was standing twenty feet away from the porch, which most people in the village would have considered a safe distance. As usual Alicia's mother threw out her curses along with the slop from her bucket, covering José's head with dishwater and peels. José didn't dare respond because he felt Alicia's mother would one day see that he was seriously in love. Alicia couldn't help but laugh at the sight, which was better than television or the movies could offer because this was a live show. Her mother threatened him with castration, and the poor young man quickly vanished in the dark, perhaps afraid that prayers and curses might come true.

-2-

Advice From a Mother

For years Alicia had lived with the dream her mother had instilled in her. As the seasons passed Alicia shed layers of skin like a lizard molting in the sand. Many of the girls at school thought she had become beautiful to spite them and were jealous of her new tongue. Whenever she got angry at them she would cry out words such as broccoli, spinach or asparagus—curse words that worked well as long as they weren't understood.

Many of the envious girls began to dream of crossing the river and finding a man that would love them as they were, but as soon as they began getting too close to Alicia, their boyfriends and mothers pulled them off. All of a sudden, Alicia had the plague.

"Aren't we good enough for you?" the men would ask.

"No!" Alicia would answer swiftly.

"You come from the same dirt," they would yell.

"But you remain in the dirt," she would cry out madly.

"We could kill you!"

"That's all you men ever say when you can't have what you want!"

Alicia Maravilla

Alicia remained on the porch alone with her cassette recorder until she finished all two hundred lessons, in the last of which Alicia had to learn how to transfer from subway to bus to get to the Metropolitan Museum of Art by getting lost near Central Park. Lucky for her she didn't take the normal detour that might have allowed her to see the homeless lying on benches taking in the sun. Lucky for her she didn't get raped. A policeman with a kind face stood at the entrance of the park and personally escorted her. His blue eyes were warm and his voice gentle.

Alicia's own departure was now set. Tomorrow she would leave this desert village where chickens clucked themselves to sleep and were too lazy to even think of laying eggs. Chickens here turned lizard and cursed the feathers on their backs. Chickens became vultures and dreamed of being eggs again. Dogs here had no names and roamed the streets and alleys with children who would not remember their names until they became men. They ran in fear of the sticks and stones thrown in anger. They trusted no hand, no man, no woman or child, especially children. They were not man's best friends.

Night had again swallowed the sun and given birth to a pale moon. Alicia's name was on the tip of everyone's tongue. Tonight they forgot their ill feelings, and Alicia was bouncing from tongue to tongue like a fly alone in the desert sand. Tonight they killed her with kind words. Many hoped she would make it across the river and bring back the amulet that would change their lives. Many hoped Alicia would find the rich blue-eyed millionaire her mother had dreamed for her.

"Who cares?"

"We care!"

"Care about what?"

"He can be brown-eyed as long as he has a million!"

"Or two."

"Or blind!"

14

S. Lecomte

"Blind millionaires have money too."
"And do you think all blind men are millionaires, José?"
"What kind of twisted logic do you have in your head?"
"Maybe all millionaires are blind?"
"Who cares? As long as he has the money."

Tonight they built a bridge to cross the river and sent Alicia on her way. Tonight they built new houses and exchanged their peasant clothes for suits and tuxedos and went to an old-fashioned dance. Refrigerators, televisions, VCRs, rifles, mink coats, alligator purses and other goodies rolled out of their mouths so that they could survive in this world. What was a man without an antenna to guide him on his journey here on earth? He was a lost sheep who needed a shepherd. All antennas lead to one station and unite men and women all over the world. The antennas, like billions of crucifixes fixed on top of their roofs, were their salvation. The antennas freed their spirits and made them hungrier for the goods the Great Spirit flashed on the screens.

Tonight Alicia, often maligned and even despised, became close to their patron saint, which they had forgotten existed. She gave them hope.

Tonight José stood at her bedroom window and wept like a drunken man wishing to revive the dead. He threatened her with his own fears. He warned her that the lessons that seemed so rosy on paper might turn out badly. Having stood by her porch like a worshipper listening to the liturgy, he picked up words like roast beef, wine, and man. He had more than the birdbrains Alicia attributed to him, and he could figure out that a woman had to pay for the wine and roast beef with her own body. He then threatened to follow her so that he could keep an eye on her and protect her. Not getting a response from her, he threatened to kill himself to prove that he was the only one in this world truly capable of loving her. José's shad-

15

ow even waved a pistol in the air to make his point. When he threatened to pull the trigger, Alicia's face appeared at the window.

Alicia's face shone in the moonlight, and José must have thought that her heart had softened. José, however, was unaware that the lessons had taught her not to respect a weak man. She had decided that she would need a man certain of himself, a man who would never think of suicide as a way to a woman's heart.

"José, put the gun down or you'll shoot someone who doesn't deserve it. If you want to shoot yourself, it's okay by me. But don't do it in front of our house. Go to the river and make sure you fall in it after you shoot yourself."

"You have such a cold heart, Alicia. You used to be so soft when you were a girl. You don't really care if I shoot myself, do you?"

"José, if you want to shoot yourself, it's up to you, not up to me. All you men . . . "

"There you go again with all you men . . . I am José, one man!"

"Okay, you one man down there, don't depend on me to define your life. And don't shoot yourself, José. You'll find a nice woman who can give you children."

"I want you!"

"Good-night, José!"

José didn't stay where he wasn't wanted and did exactly as he had been ordered to. Tonight he went to the river and shot his pistol. Someone heard a shot fired by the river. Someone had seen José try to shoot himself again and dismissed the image as a rerun. José thought he would make Alicia see how she affected men and was floating downriver like a piece of brown driftwood. It would be days before his body would be found ashore, days after Alicia had left. It would be a year or maybe less before Alicia would find out the news, which would be old and stale when she would hear it. Justice would be served by the police who would find José's brother Ignacio guilty of the crime because he had threatened to kill him for a lousy rooster that had been castrated and decapitated out of José's frustration. People thought, better the rooster than José. He would be buried and quickly forgotten, his name living among the many faces, some of who were also named José.

As soon as José disappeared, Rosita came and stood by Alicia's window and prayed to her as if she were part of an altar. Rosita had learned a good twenty lessons with Alicia's help. Now she too wanted to taste roast beef and drink champagne even though she had not yet finished any of the lessons that led to the restaurant in New York.

Alicia heard Rosita peeping and felt sorry for her as she usually did. Her face was covered with dirt and her only dress so worn out that it might fall off her body any minute. Alicia knew why she had come, and before Rosita could open her mouth, Alicia told her she couldn't come with her. Rosita cried but didn't blame Alicia, but she too would follow in the distance. Alicia told her how dangerous it would be for a child to cross the desert and the river. She quickly replied, "I'm as much a woman as you. I can take care of myself!"

"Rosita, please, come back. Rosita, don't be mad at me!"

Rosita vanished into the darkness in pursuit of José, whom she had loved in secrecy. But Rosita remained among the living and would wait for Alicia's return if Alicia ever left the village.

Actually many of the people in the village had begun to have their doubts about Alicia ever leaving this part of the world. It even seemed that the vultures had grown impatient over the years as they too watched Alicia listening to her lessons. They too thought she was ready to leave home in search of the man from her mother's dream.

Tonight was the night.

As she lay dreaming of the man she had yet to define because she lacked any real concrete image, her mother's squatty body entered her room and sat down like a large hen come to cluck advice Alicia had always resented but heeded. She felt her mother's hand caress her cheek as if this were the last time they would see each other. Not one to drag things out, her mother told her what to expect across the river.

Her mother had led her to believe that the streets across the river were paved with gold stolen from the Indians long ago and that the trees yielded not fruit but money, and with money you could buy as much fruit as you wanted.

"But if only money grows on trees, Mamá, what can you buy?"

"Of course, they have special trees that grow fruit. Do you think they would only grow one type of tree? People would starve if they only had money and no food to eat."

"We would have food to eat, Mamá!"

"Alicia, I hear the voice of uncertainty."

"No, Mamá. I will go and find a husband who will provide for us all, but I want to be in love when I do."

"In love? I was in love!"

Her mother had been in love several times. At the age of twelve she gave birth to Alicia in a goat pen. The boy, José Hernandez, had offered her candy, licorice, her favorite, and she had opened her legs for him so that he could peek at the secret of life. The next minute before she knew it, he brought out his tiny snake and put it in her. José promised to marry her when they got older, but as soon as he saw her belly growing like a melon basking in the sun, drinking from the dry earth, José vanished across the river and was never seen again. The only remnant of this boy was a picture of him when he was ten and a seventeen-year old Alicia.

Her mother had also loved the bank robber who had promised her a mansion by the sea and all the fish she could

eat. Her lover was shot. She had also had a bout with the Holy
Spirit and Father Romero, whose penis was not only the thick-
est but the longest snake in the village. Father Romero
promised her Heaven and absolution from all sins in which he
had stopped believing years ago. Rosario was born. She didn't
know who Rosario's father was, and this would lead to
Rosario's confusion.

There had been others who paid her in children and
chickens until one day she decided that men were only out to
use the female flesh like gods hungry to quench their discon-
tentment here on earth. Rosa had gone across the river three
months ago. The unnamed one was born dead and spared a
diet of frijoles. Victor was carried off downriver during a flood
five years ago and his body was never recovered.

After the death of the unnamed one, she decided she
would like to live the life of a nun. Because of her miserable
luck with men, whom she always referred to as boys, she
defended Alicia's virginity like a dragon blowing fire through
nostrils every time young men came sniffing around like dogs
at their own piss.

At rutting season the young men seemed to be on fire,
yearning to enter the females, mouths filled with promises and
words that didn't come from their hearts. Alicia's mother,
known as la bruja loca (crazy witch) stood on her porch with
a broom and beat the young men off like flies and bees looking for something sour and something sweet. For years she
threw water, rocks, anything she could get her hands on, but
the dogs continued to come and sniff and howl and moan in
pain, claiming their balls were hurting because of the love
inflating them. The rocks had never hit any of the young men
because she was a bad shot. Only when she killed Alejandro
Ramirez Cabeza de Vaca, after hitting him on what was
known to be a stubborn bullish head, did the young men take
her threats seriously.

Alicia, who had also felt the urge to sneak out in the night like a female coyote in heat, was kept on a leash by her mother to teach her logic. Her mother tied her to the bed with a rope once, and Alicia untied it, but fortunately for her, she was caught with her skirt up while the boy was only unbuckling his pants. Her mother went wild with rage and the broom. Miguel Alvarez de la Puta was found bleeding in the cemetery. Most believed that certain ghosts from his family's past had risen to avenge their honor because the de la Puta family was the richest in the province after robbing the peasants throughout history. Miguel Alvarez de la Puta deserved the punishment from beyond. Meanwhile Alicia's bottom was so sore she couldn't sit down for weeks.

Of course, like all the martyrs, she promised never to go out the window again and was repentant only as long as she felt the pain of her mother's wrath from the broomstick. Alicia felt like a wild mare imprisoned by la bruja loca and escaped several more times only to be saved from perdition and pregnancy by the sound of her mother's broom and her screeching voice that tore through the skies like a mad goddess, demanding vengeance for crimes committed against nature itself.

Alicia's yearning for a young man came to a sudden halt the day she realized she was the most beautiful woman in the village. This piece of vanity saved her belly from getting impregnated by some wormy-looking penis, and she was grateful to her mother that she had remained a virgin. Now that she looks back she doesn't understand why she was so stupid.

Many of the girls at school accused her of having a cold heart. They claimed she was dead and should never have been born if she couldn't feel a man's lips against hers. And she was definitely afraid of life if she didn't allow herself to be mounted by a young buck. Now that she listened through the night she was happy she wasn't one of them sitting on the porch hitting her children to keep them away like flies. She was happy her breasts were intact and not flowing with milk, a poison that perpetuated life as it was, a life of poverty, a life of misery.

Alicia had been listening to the night and its plaintive voices before her mother had come in. Another boy had been born to María next door and this life was killing María. She would die several days after Alicia's departure and the father would die drunk several months down the road, after being robbed. And the boy would be baptized and sent to an orphanage run by Franciscan monks. This young Father Romero would return to his native village twenty-three years later and continue the legacy of the now dearly departed Father Romero. The rumor was that he had dropped dead on top of some young woman as everyone had expected. But he had died during confession listening to sins he never heard. God forbid these sins should be written down or Father Romero might have come to life again. Actually, the sins had not caused his heart to be upset, but the piece of chuleta (porkchop) he had been eating did when it became lodged in his throat preventing him from breathing. The sinner in the booth, a woman of some repute, ill in the eyes of other sinners, was blamed for all the excitement and put in jail for murder. The laws of the country were clear. Words were to be weighed before spoken. She was eventually raped by several guards and freed. She accepted the rape as something natural but never went to confession again as long as she lived.

Alicia was glad she didn't go to confession either and thanked her mother for her love and lack of restraint. Any child in those more civilized countries would have accused her mother of child abuse, but Alicia was grateful for the sore bottom she was now proud of. How many unabused children could claim the same? How many were virgins? Their mothers must have talked to them until they turned blue in the face, but they didn't love their children or they would have used her mother's broom.

Alicia thanked her mother for the chicken, frijoles, tortillas. She thanked her for the many well-deserved beatings. And how proud she felt that she was almost the only virgin in the village! She was grateful to her mother for the wonderful tapes and the dream that was to come true once she crossed the river.

No matter how much a mother loves her daughter, she cannot allow her to dribble stupidities out of her mouth even if those words and thoughts originated from her mother's mouth in the first place.

"Alicia, please, pay attention to what I'm going to say."

"Mamá, you sound so displeased."

"I am displeased with myself for not telling you the truth."

"You are my mother, aren't you?"

"Yes."

"And the boy José Hernandez is my father?"

"Yes! Why the stupid questions?"

"Because I thought you were going to tell me that Father Romero was my father too."

"You are my daughter."

"Thank God!"

"The tapes and books weren't printed in Heaven, Alicia."

"I know, Mamá. They were printed in New York."

"I'm not speaking literally, Alicia. What I'm trying to say is that people are the same everywhere you go. There is violence everywhere."

"I know, Mamá."

"I thought you might have forgotten because of the wine, roast beef, beaches, hotels and the many nice people you met."

"They were nice, and I think most of them are nice because they are rich, Mamá. I think people treat each other like dogs because they don't have enough to eat."

"How smart you are, Alicia!"

Her mother, like Shakespeare's Polonius, spent the night giving her advice. Alicia was to trust only men with blue eyes. Those belonged to men across the river, to northern men, whose tempers were restrained, whose manners were polished, and whose pockets were lined with silver and bellies were full of money. Women with blue eyes and blond hair were jealous and had cold hearts. Her mother told Alicia about la norteamericana from Boston, but that was another story. Men with brown eyes were no better than goats. They stank, had no backbone, had no manners and could never be taught to have any. These men-goats could only bellow in pain, their penises inflamed because of love. Alicia was to trust no man who told her he loved her right away.

Alicia was not to set her goals high. The man could be stupid and have a lot of money. It didn't matter because men and women couldn't really talk to one another anyway. A stupid man could be sent out to sleep with hogs and he wouldn't know the difference.

Alicia was to keep her heart in check and not allow it to weaken. Men have fancy ways. She was to play it humble but not give herself away. She was supposed to be the honey and they the bees. Once she found the right bee, she was not allowed to let him sting her. She was supposed to trap him in the jar full of honey and close the lid tight to teach him his place. Then she was supposed to bring the bee and honey home.

The tall blue-eyed young man with pale skin with roast beef on the tip of his tongue vanished across the river. She could hear his kind and loving words until her mother told her that she should, by no means, give away her virginity to any man until he signed his name beside hers.

She was to respect everyone she met, take advantage of no one and not allow anyone to take advantage of her. The rest would come naturally, and if she should ever be in doubt of her feelings, her mother asked her to think of her and the broom that often grazed her bottom. Even from across the river her mother would be able to save her.

-3-
The Beginnings

The morning Alicia left, everyone came out to wish her well, and all hoped she would find what she was after. Seeing all the people so full of concern as they had never been, she couldn't change her mind even if she wanted to, which she didn't. After embraces from almost everyone in the village, she felt exhausted and would have gone back to bed had her mother not hit her with the broom for good luck and good measure.

The sun was rising from the east. The sky filled with blood as the mountains rose from their sleep. Mourning doves were cooing, perched on the many roofs. She walked ahead with no map, no plan of action, just a dream that was to come true. The voices in back of her died down.

When she finally turned around, many of the small figures had disappeared and only her mother and Rosario were still waving like two small flowers blowing in the wind. At this point she felt tears moisten her dry cheeks. She had the sudden urge to go back and have breakfast, which she had missed because everyone had been in a hurry to send her off to see how quickly she could come back. Some of those who owned a television set wanted instant solutions. They wanted to know immediately what kind of a man she would bring back. Alicia continued on the road that led to the river.

The sun had risen and the road of asphalt shimmered like an open sea ready to swallow up cars and trucks, which hardly traveled this road. The heat was getting hotter, and in her mind she imagined the snow and little Christmas man riding through the sky across the river. She had watched television several times without her mother's knowledge, and she was glad snow existed where she was going. Unfortunately, Alicia had watched a series on Alaska and was under the impression that all of the United States and Canada were constantly covered with ice and snow.

As the sun grew hotter, the mountains seemed to wave like spirits. She knelt in the shade of a saguaro cactus like a jackrabbit and stayed there for a while. She drank some water and wiped her face with a wet rag. As she sat in the shade, Alicia watched a large green lizard flicking its tongue. At first she thought it was mocking her, but then she noticed it was snapping insects as they came out of a dead cactus. Full of ants, the lizard scurried a while and then lay down on the skeleton of a tree and began basking in the sun. No sooner had it spread its limbs than a hawk fell out of the sky like vengeance from God and snatched the lizard up as if it had never been, taking it and the ants for a ride into its own belly. The hawk soared up and landed on top of a cactus where it shredded the lizard, shaking it like a silent bell.

Although Alicia felt like sleeping, she told herself that dreams do not come true in sleep. She continued walking along the road, her head full of imaginary heads. An elegant store she had once seen in a glamour magazine stood at the end of the road. Many men and women in fancy and colorful clothing stood at counters buying whatever they wanted. She too walked into the store. At first she felt timid, trying to formulate a grammatically correct phrase that wouldn't arouse their laughter. She had heard that these people laughed at others even when they were helpless.

Alicia walked to one of the counters and asked to see a catalogue of men. The saleswoman, a tall brunette with claws dipped in blood, opened her mouth caked with blood and showed her fangs. She hissed at her in a strange language and began laughing. Everyone then took up the laughter. Alicia was frightened! Had she learned the wrong language? Did the people across the river not speak English? When the laughter abated, the saleswoman opened her bloody mouth and spoke the English she had learned on the tapes. Alicia was relieved.

"Dearie, you should know a few things about life. What did your mother teach you anyway? First of all, you'll never find a decent man, dressed as a tramp the way you are. And I mean tramp as bum, poverty stricken and poor, dearie. Put this on."

Dressed in a black décolleté, Alicia looked like a ripe fleshy fruit ready to be plucked from the tree it grew on. She looked at her body in the mirror and decided that she was more beautiful than before.

"Dearie, don't get too many fancy ideas in your head. You can't think you're the most beautiful. There are always new models that'll come and replace you. Here, let's make up your face. This cherry red for your lips. A dash of blue for your eyes. Now you are ready for the husband of the century sale. The problem is, dearie, there are no whole men left. Women here don't like what they have. So they make everything up and reshape what they don't like. It's a matter of image."

The saleswoman with bloody claws took Alicia down into a dark cellar, turned the lights on and said, "This is where you pick the man's head. Pay attention, dearie, because you can never replace the brain once it's put into the skull."

The walls were lined with men's heads. There were blondes, brunettes, redheads, and bald heads. There were some with blue eyes, brown eyes, and green eyes. Some had long noses. Others short, stubby, pug noses. There were wide mouths. Thin lips, thick lips. Their features confused Alicia. Some showed their tongues in jest. Others acted stupid. Some said nothing. Others tried to seem intelligent. Alicia couldn't just choose a man's head without the body.

"They don't look like men to me," Alicia said quietly so as not to be heard.

"Dearie, you'll have to learn that the body isn't everything."

"It would be nice to see one of them walk and dance. Can they dance and sing?"

"These men do dance and sing, but they need bodies for that, but before they can be given bodies, you must choose a head."

"How can I choose a head without a body? I cannot choose parts of a man."

"Dearie, that's the way things are done here. You came here to find a man with money, right?"

"Yes."

"You came to the wrong store. These men are for sale. You need to find a man in real life."

"Here are your clothes back."

"Keep them. You'll need them."

The hawk soared above her as if trying to say something she would need to understand later on, but its voice was drowned by the winds that move the clouds. A truck honked its horn and almost hit her. The brakes screeched and several men with dark brown coyote faces surrounded her. Their breaths smelled of tequila, and their words were not their own. Their mouths opened like strange traps, their lips ejecting filthy words she had heard all her life. But these filthy words coming from the mouths of strangers frightened her. They all began touching her, at first playfully. She withdrew from their filthy hands, but other hands grabbed her violently. One of them held her against himself and began kissing her. Another had taken his pants down. Alicia screamed for help and then bit her captor on the hand. She hit the man with the exposed penis in the belly and ran.

Alicia ran into the desert away from the road, thinking the wilderness much safer than civilized roads. As soon as she was out of sight among the saguaro forest and mesquite bushes, she hid behind a boulder. The hawk fell out of the wind like a kite and landed on one of the coyote men's heads. Its claws were piercing the coyote's eyes. The void was suddenly filled with pain—the pain Alicia might have felt herself. She was glad the coyote was crying out. It would teach him to respect women and other beings. As the pain was absorbed by the hills and the desert sand, Alicia continued to walk away from the road, her feet sinking in the sand, the heat sapping her strength from above and below.

As she trudged uphill in the direction of the river, she thanked the Virgin Mary even though she had hardly gone to church. Prayers once instilled in childhood had no escape from her head. Alicia had once thought of becoming a nun, but that had been a fleeting thought. All she would have done would have been to pray and beg in the streets so as to feed the poor.

A ferret was climbing in a mesquite bush in search of nests and eggs. Several doves were digging into the red seeds of the saguaro cactus. A jackrabbit lay still in the shade. A shot resounded in the distance, and the hawk that had protected her, fell out of the skies. The truck on the road turned around and drove towards the village that could no longer be seen from where she was. Alicia felt sorrow in her heart, not only for the dead hawk now probably covered with ants, but also for herself. She would have to be wary of all men, and never buy a man's head or body. Poor men could always be bought. Poor men have no real love in their hearts! Poor men can only rape to make themselves feel rich. At this point Alicia hated all poor men because of the incident at the roadside and the many fights and violent deaths she had experienced in her village.

The deeper she went into the desert, the more she realized that death ruled life and not the other way around. Yet near the skull of a long-dead cow she saw a small group of yellow flowers with petals so fragile that she was amazed for the first time in her life. She had seen these yellow nameless flowers before but had never asked herself how they survived in this harsh desert climate. But why did the people in her village stay here? They were not flowers and had legs to carry them to other places. The soil was poor and yielded a poor harvest. The river swelled in the spring and carried off people's houses and livestock. The heat was at times unbearable. But everyone stayed rooted like the flowers to the ground that had given birth to them and would claim them when they died. No matter how poor the land was, it was theirs, and the land owned them.

As she walked she stopped to watch another horned lizard snapping ants and eating them as they came out of their sandy hill. Death did give life to the desert. She thought of the villagers lying in the sand and waiting for the cool nights to soothe their bones. She remembered sitting in the cemetery once, praying to the man she thought had been her father. After a while she heard voices come from beneath her. Men and women laughed in a wild and happy manner unheard of in the village. If there was laughter before death, it was one of despair. But these dead men and women were laughing with genuine happiness.

Alicia had remained calm, not wanting to disturb their state. The night had been still and blue, the coyotes asleep, the moon dead in some other orbit. Then she had heard music as if it were coming from the stars. Then Emiliano came out of his grave and sat next to her. She wasn't frightened by the sight of his figure as she should have been. She even allowed him to hold her hand.

Alicia recalled Emiliano's dying days and how full of hope he had been. Emiliano used to disappear for weeks, sometimes months, and then come back to the village as if resurrected every time he returned because many had thought him dead. Emiliano would make his rounds and tell his stories of adventures met on the road. At times he had been beaten and robbed of what he didn't possess. He made love to beauties he said grew in the desert. Many thought the beauties grew in his mind, but Alicia liked to think that love was possible, even after death.

One day Emiliano came back with a wonderful adventure he had met on a river raft. After days of floating, he rescued a young woman from drowning and revived her. She was so grateful to him that she slashed his face for not allowing her to die. Since she had wanted to die, Emiliano pushed her back into the river. As she floated downriver she thanked him. Everyone in the village laughed and thought this story was better than the fish stories he used to tell.

One day Emiliano told Alicia how unappreciated he was as a storyteller. People laughed when he wanted to be taken seriously. Emiliano had traveled the river and highways; he had crossed the desert and climbed the many hills and mountains. He had kissed the snake on its cold lips and drunk of its venom. He had flown on the wings of the hawk and eaten with the condors. Emiliano was sadly underrated, and he would make them pay by never returning.

One night Emiliano got drunk and walked out of the village unseen by anyone. In the morning they found his body shot through and through. Some said he committed suicide, even though they found no gun next to him. The same said Emiliano wished the gun away after he shot himself. Others claimed Emiliano talked too much and were fed up with old-fashioned stories and that he was shot because he wouldn't let them watch television in peace. Yet others said that he had witnessed drug smuggling operations in the hills near the river and that he was shot before he could go to the police who were as crooked as the drug smugglers.

Emiliano was alive and well on the tip of people's tongues. They were even thinking about erecting a monument to his memory for all the stories he had told. The monument would speak of Emiliano's greatness and of course of the village's glory. Emiliano's stories were now the history of the village through which the people had lived. The monument was the spirit of the village. It would be placed on a map and tourists would flock like vultures to carrion, peck a while with their cameras, sniff at the burro shit a while and never return. Emiliano, now the name of the village, would live forever.

No sooner had Alicia finished her last thought than she noticed what she imagined to be a mirage. As she approached it, she realized that the walls were real and white as the sand and adobe they were made of. There were several houses and an abandoned mission whose cross seemed to dangle in the now lazy sky. She cried out the usual, "Is anybody home?" knowing that this village had died with the dry riverbed below. She went into the mission where the air was cool.

Alicia sat down and drank some water from the gourd she was carrying. The water came alive in her throat like a river sent throughout her body to give life to the cells that might have dried up like rocks turned to sand. Water was the resurrection Christ had talked about. Without water everything in

the world would die. Alicia noticed the absence of religious
regalia and imagined a priest, perhaps unlike Father Romero,
taking Christ down from his cross and telling Him he was free
to go back into the desert to look for more water. Christ was
given some rags and a sombrero and a divining stick. These
villagers waited for Him to return, hoping to be saved by the
Savior, but He didn't return. Only people can make miracles
happen, her mother told her often. Then she would cross herself several times, even though she had stopped going to
church.

The sky soon grew somber and grey through the roof, long
fallen from the rafters. The air became cool quickly and Alicia
shivered in a corner of the mission like the jackrabbit in the
corner across from her. She spoke to it out of compassion for
herself and the sudden loneliness she was feeling. Perhaps she
should have stayed home and given in to José, whose face was
still glued to her window and begging for her hand in marriage. Out of these surroundings, she felt a horrible terror! She
was alone, on her own at the mercy of the sun, night, and men
who might harm her! Night frightened her as it had never
done before. Out here she was game like the rest of the animals. Lucky for her, she thought, she was no ant for the lizard's
belly. After she comforted herself, she decided to give up José
to Rosita who truly loved him even if José didn't love her. The
two would marry out of boredom, and José would learn to
beat Rosita in Alicia's memory and they would have lots of
children, one of whom might be named after her. Alicia was
unaware of José's suicide.

Alicia erased José and the village from her mind as she
tried to recite several of her lessons by heart. Many of the
lessons had dealt with foods of various types. As she sat in several restaurants, she was served fish, shrimp, gumbo, roast
beef, lamb, pork chops, potato au gratin, asparagus and an
assortment of desserts that made her palate wet for food. Her

stomach began to ache and all of a sudden she felt like a prisoner in a jail where they offered food as torture. Poor people were offered food through new television sets, but couldn't taste any of it. Her mother had preferred no television and had satisfied her belly with frijoles and tortillas. With the English lessons she had studied, Alicia's belly had begun yearning for something different. The words had to be tasted before she could know what they meant. She set her mind on the man she was to find. But the more she thought about his features, the more she got confused. This put her to sleep.

No sooner had she fallen asleep than she was awakened by a tall woman in a long light blue robe. She was carrying a bouquet of roses in her arm and her mouth and eyes were bright with light. Her voice was gentle yet stern as she addressed Alicia.

"Alicia, do not be frightened by my appearance. I have come to you out of love for you and your mother. I have come because Emiliano was worried about you. I know you must find a husband who will save you and the village, but be careful not to be too hasty. Money isn't everything, Alicia. And men with different blood do not always respect women of your type. Even cows do not drink from a pig's trough. Even the water you may drink from the same cup will taste different. Men are the same, yet the same men are different. They fool easily. They will open their mouths unwillingly and will pronounce their love as if you were the last woman on earth. Be gentle with them, but do not give in to them. Have a good trip."

In the morning Alicia awoke with a rose in her hand. She should have been surprised, but she had had so many visitations at the cemetery that such so-called miracles had become almost routine. Instead, she felt the helping hand of someone who would not abandon her. Yet, when she would reach the river, the woman in blue would appear to her one last time and in a sad voice announce that spirits from this side of the river could not go across because the land was as different as its people.

Alicia was on her own.

-4-

Crossing the River

Exhausted and disappointed by the lack of snow on the other side, Alicia reached the river she was to cross. She sat down and caught her breath for a while as she took in the scene like an explorer coming from civilization into the wilderness. The land seemed sandy with cactus and vultures on the other side, and the sky was as blue and cloudless as back in her village. Had the books she had read been wrong about the snow? She flipped through the pages in her mind and noticed the absence of tall mountains. She thought she had perhaps taken the wrong road and should have stayed on the main highway. Had Alicia paid attention in school when history was taught, she might have known that the land north of the river once belonged to her country and that was the reason why the land looked the same.

As she climbed down the hill, however, the sameness slowly dissipated like morning dew, and she noticed how green the land across the river really was in comparison to the land she was standing on. There were orange, lemon, and grapefruit trees lacking on her side of the river. The land across seemed to smile and welcome the poor and unfortunate. Alicia thought she might need a drink of water to wake up from the pleasant dream she thought she was having.

The closer she came to the river, the happier she became. She had reached her goal, and everything and everyone who had occupied her thoughts vanished like bats frightened by daylight. After cooling her face and neck, she walked downriver to find a shallow place where she might cross. There were voices in her own language around the bend.

As she came around she could see several boys with no shirts or shoes running towards her with oranges in their shirts. Two large black dogs, of a breed she had never seen, were running after them but gave up the chase at the water's edge. The boys, three in all, were apparently from a neighboring village on this side of the river, and they raided the orange groves in the distance before taking their harvest to the local market on their side of the river. Their faces glowed with mischief and self-satisfaction. Their eyes shone like the evening light. They were sated with victory, their bellies filling up with the pride of stolen oranges as they ate with delight. "To steal from those who have is a blow for justice," the tallest of them exclaimed to her.

"Why don't you go across and find a job like many have done?" Alicia asked.

"Hey, how old are you? What's in your head anyway? Pumpkin seeds or something?" the tallest said like a man who had traveled the four corners of the earth.

The runt of the group, a wall-eyed boy with almost no teeth stepped up to the leader of the pack and said, "Maybe she's not from around here."

"Maybe she just fell out of the sky?" the tallest asked, laughing alone.

The medium-sized boy offered her one of the stolen oranges and quickly released it in her hand. Then he moved towards the other two who were about to go uphill.

"We stay here because this is our land. Our home is here and so is our spirit. When we touch the other side for just a second we feel a great emptiness in our hearts. Once you cross the river here, you will forget your own name. We don't even drink from this river because they do," the medium-sized boy told her.

"My sister went over there several years ago, and she hasn't been back since. They say giant lizards ate her," the youngest with no teeth cried out.

"There are no such things as giant lizards. Enough of this dumb talk. As soon as you see a girl, your minds go to mush. Let's go! We have work to do!" the tall one said.

"Be careful," the medium-sized boy said, "Be careful! As you cross the river continue to repeat your name. Mine's Pepe. And I live on the other side of that hill. If you need a place to stay, my parents wouldn't mind. Just ask for the Delicados. Remember, keep repeating your name or they will take it from you. Good luck!"

The three boys continued on their journey uphill. They would return tomorrow and every day until the season or harvest was done. Then they would disappear and migrate with the birds to more fertile fields and orchards and return next year. They vanished over the steep bank, and she was alone with the two black dogs waiting for her across the way.

Undaunted by their snarling and gnashing teeth, she took her first step into the water. As she walked across, she kept repeating her name as if it were a sacred prayer. When she reached the other side, she opened her eyes to the dogs barking for their master to notice what they had caught. Their barking grew louder as she moved away from them. As soon as they heard a whistle, they quieted down and were replaced by a thin woman with a beak for a nose and small sharp eyes that seemed to cut right through her. The thin woman yelled some curses and waved her broom in the air like a witch frustrated with her mode of transportation.

"They don't make brooms the way they used to. Vacuums work better," Alicia said, recalling an ad on brooms and vacuums from one of her English lessons.

Aware of the broom, the thin woman put it down. Her eyes examined Alicia up, down, across, as if she were ribs ready to be barbecued. Then unsatisfied with what she hadn't found as evidence of thievery, she prodded Alicia with the broomstick, searched her pockets and underskirts. Still she could find nothing.

"You people are all the same. You're like locusts sent by the devil to ruin this land. We made it heavenly and you come to ruin it. I have watered and nurtured every tree in this orchard, and I am sick of your brothers coming over and stealing what's not theirs. The Lord said, 'Thou shalt not steal!' You people do go to church, don't you? What do they teach you there?"

Alicia remained mute, unable to answer the thin woman, whose words had been fired like bullets out of a machine gun. The bullets had been meant to kill, not to wound, but she was still alive because many of the words had confused her. Alicia figured that the devil had asked this poor woman to steal from a tree and she had become sick because of it. Alicia, however, had heard that story before, but her mother had told her not to believe every word she heard, especially words coming from the mouth of Father Romero. Her mother had warned her that men had invented untrue stories about women to keep them as low as the snake that crawls forever damned because of its nasty tongue. And after defending women from men, her mother would light into women for their foul mouths.

The thin woman led Alicia towards three men near a black pot smoking with ribs covered with tomato sauce. One of the men had an Adam's apple the size of a lemon. He looked like an unshaven buzzard with a small cowboy hat. He was the first of the men to notice Alicia.

"Whatch ye got dere, Mae. Purty lookin' heifer. What's yer name, honey?"

"She's no heifer and she isn't your honey, Mr. Austin."

"Do you always half to do dat? Just 'cause we ain't got dat damned Bible under our belt, don't mean we're stupid!" the obese man with the turnip nose cried out like a puppy whose voice had been arrested in adolescence. Alicia had read somewhere that young boys were once castrated so that they could sing like girls.

"Ace, all I want you and your friends to do is respect people, especially women."

"What's yer name? Now is that a proper question?"

"Alicia."

"That's a purty name if you ast me."

"Nobody asked you," the thin woman told the young man who had been lying on the grass until awakened by this woman who was apparently his mother. He had the same beak and the same sharp eyes that were a shade or two grayer.

"Cain't nobody say nothin' 'round here," the boy continued.

"Mind yer Ma, boy."

"Old man, I don't have to put up with this shit!" the boy said, getting up and leaving them to decide Alicia's fate.

"If I wuz you I'd cross the river and go home," he yelled as he disappeared into the house.

The unshaven buzzard studied her with his sheep-like eyes and said, "Watch yer gonna do wit her, Mae?"

"I don't rightly know. I could use more help in the house or put her to work in the orchards picking!"

"Such a fine heifer don't belong in no orchard."

"All you got your mind on is heifers! The good Lord won't take too kindly to your thoughts, or orange thieves like her for that matter!"

"Now, Mae, everybody dat comes across this Rio Grande don't especially like oranges," the obese man said.

Alicia, immersed in a sea of words, was swimming among them, understanding only that she was being accused of stealing oranges.

"I didn't steal no orange," she said.

"She can speak," the buzzard exclaimed as if he had been surprised by an alien from outer space.

"English . . . " the obese man yelled, surprised by the fact.

"She speaks as if she were from Brooklyn."

"You don't sound no different, Mae."

"I took lessons from tapes."

"She took lessons from tapes, d'ye hear dat?" the obese man was so flabbergasted that he couldn't help but laugh and fart himself silly.

"Mind your manners, Ace!"

"A man's gotta fart when he's gotta fart, Mae," the buzzard said.

"You could at least have waited until we've eaten."

The dogs began yelping as the smell of barbecued meat rose through the air and settled like pollen in their nostrils. The obese man picked out several ribs and threw them to the dogs. They began gnawing at the bones like cannibals eating their own kind. The buzzard picked out some corn and ribs and said, "I bet she's hungry. Cain't let a heifer like dat fade away. It's got to be fed or it won't bring in a decent price on the market!"

"I bet she's hungry. That's why she came across to steal our oranges!"

"Will ye let dem oranges go a'ready?" the obese man peeped like a chick trying to be a rooster before its time.

"I'll feed her inside away from your gawking eyes!"

As soon as the thin woman led Alicia inside the house, the buzzard and the obese man continued their conversation, untainted by the thin woman's interfering presence. Since Alicia would not have understood their words, it might not be a bad idea to relate them to make them clear.

"Dems good roastin' ears, Ace."

"Austin, I just plum don't know what de hell to do wit dat boy o' mine. He don't have as much sense as you could slap in a gnat's ass with a butter paddle."

"I agree wit ye, Ace, if his brains was dynamite he wouldn't have enough to blow his nose."

"I mean he's so lazy he stops plowin' to fart."

"He won't amount to a hill of beans, but he does have good taste in women."

"Yeh, but he's always layin' out wit the dry cattle."

"He's like a calf kicking yeller jackets."

"Wild as a boar in a peach orchard, ye mean."

"He's got to learn this ain't no playground."

"Cain't do much wit him now!"

Should Alicia have heard this conversation, she would have been confused. Lucky for her she had been taken inside to be fed by this apparent Christian woman who prided herself on the fact that she was saving heathens from perdition by showing them that her religion, based on charity, was better than any other. The Lord, she would mention to Alicia in passing, had spoken to her personally and had told her that she would get to Heaven if she brought in His flock to be baptized into the Baptist Church. Alicia thought that perhaps God had changed His own religion once He crossed the river. What was the difference?

Ready to taste the food of charity from this thin God-loving woman who seemed very unhappy with her life, Alicia opened her mouth when she walked into the kitchen. It was a large room with many counters and cupboards. There were many jars filled with many things: coffee, sugar, flour, red, white and yellow beans. There were canned jellies, green beans, baby corn. There were salted hams hanging on hooks from the ceiling. There were baskets filled with bread, rolls, apples, bananas, oranges, lemons, grapefruit, and cantaloupes. Alicia knew their names from the pictures she had seen, but they were unknown to her palate and therefore the communion was still incomplete. Once she tasted them the words would die and so would the mystery.

Alicia was dying to taste an orange, a banana, a slice of cantaloupe, a bite of an apple. No sooner had she awakened her craving than she heard the thin woman's compassionate Christian voice ask, "Are you a God-fearing woman, Alicia?"

"Yes," Alicia answered, although she had not understood the words God-fearing to its full extent even though she knew God and fear as separate entities. Her mother had often told her to answer in the affirmative when in doubt.

Pleased by Alicia's answer, the thin woman said, "I bet you must be hungry!"

"Yes," Alicia answered calmly so as not to show her enthusiasm. There was, after all, decorum to uphold, and she wasn't about to act like a dog that has gone without food for days.

"He who does not work does not eat," the thin woman said.

Alicia was somewhat baffled by the entire event and words she wished she had understood completely.

The thin woman stared at Alicia's puzzled face and explained as slowly and loudly as she could that nothing came free in this life or in the hereafter. Seeing that she had not understood a word she had explained in perfect English, the thin woman showed her a dishrag and dirty dishes.

"Nice dishes," Alicia said.

"Yes, they are. My grandmother brought them out here from New York when this place was still wilderness. Not that's it's changed any."

"Do you have roast beef? I do prefer asparagus instead of spinach," Alicia said pointing to a banana. "But a banana will do," she added enunciating each word as if she were trying to teach the thin woman her own language.

"Arrogant little bitch! You understood everything I said before! You will never make an ass out of me again!"

Alicia couldn't understand why the thin woman was creating such a fuss over asparagus and a banana. After all, had she not asked if she was hungry? She had. Or was this woman so cruel that she had offered food just to tease her palate? To avoid anymore misunderstandings, the thin woman called out Teresa's name. As quick as lightning, a small spry girl of Alicia's age popped out of the woodwork before them. She was dark with black hair. Her mouth curled with dissatisfaction at the edges like lizard tails. She seemed capricious, and her dark brown eyes had more than a tinge of jealousy as she looked at Alicia.

"Yes, Mrs. Reed."

"Teresa, this is Alicia. I want you to tell her that in my house there is no free lunch."

"Alicia, la señora says that lunch is free but not in her house."

Alicia nodded. The thin woman smiled.

"Teresa, tell her that the Bible teaches us not to be greedy. I saw the way she coveted that banana there. It is sinful to covet."

"Alicia, la señora says that the Bible is full of greedy people and that bananas are as sinful as apples."

"I didn't say manzanas. Are you translating everything I'm saying?"

"Yes, Mrs. Reed, every word."

"Tell her that Christians expect nothing from nothing."

"Alicia, I think the old woman wants you to do the dishes. And don't break any of them. They belonged to her grandmother, and if you chip one of them, she will kill you. The last girl that washed and broke one of her dishes, she had whipped naked in the yard and after the poor thing lost consciousness, she sicked the dogs on her."

"Teresa, are you through now? I mean, what did you tell her? Were you talking about me?"

"Oh no, señora, I would never talk about you. But I told her everything you expect her to know. She's going to do the dishes. I told her that!"

"Teresa, how many times have I told you not to assume?"

"I'm sorry, señora."

"Tell her she will be fed after she washes the dishes."

"You caused me problems, puta. Who asked you to come across the river? I have it made here, and now you show up!"

"Teresa, what are you saying?"

"She said you should learn Spanish, señora."

"I didn't hear her say a word, Teresa."

"That's because Spanish is a secret language, Mrs. Reed. You didn't see her lips move. She speaks without words. You must watch her careful-like."

"Just tell her to do the dishes."

"Alicia, do the dishes."

Alicia stood at the sink alone, washing each dish as if it were a precious museum piece that could cause her death if broken by accident. She wondered why Teresa appeared envious of her presence. There was something suspicious, even dangerous about her. An evil aura seemed to hang about her head like a halo, green with envy. A girl or woman whose mouth curls at the edges like lizard tails had to be watched carefully.

The thin woman sat behind Alicia who was aware of her through the smacking noises of lips and meat whose aroma penetrated Alicia's nostrils. Her stomach ached for food, her hands trembling carefully not to break any of the dishes that lay scattered in pieces in her imagination. Alicia thought that the thin woman couldn't wait for her to break a dish so that she could come alive by sinking her bony fingers into her flesh and drinking of her blood like the bats she had seen sinking their teeth into cows' necks and bellies. Alicia finished the dishes without breaking a single one. The thin woman seemed disappointed by the almost perfect washing. She examined every dish, every spoon, knife, saucer, but found no remnants of food, smudges or smears.

The thin woman didn't thank her. After all, she was the host here, not the guest. As a matter of fact, Alicia had heard that in some countries the guest thanked the host for washing dishes and other things.

"Thank you, Mrs. Reed."

"Thank me for what?"

"For allowing me the pleasure of meeting with your dishes."

"For washing them, you mean?"

"Yes, thank you for allowing me the pleasure of washing your dishes."

"Why, that's very kind of you."

"In my village we thank people when we give."

"Are you still hungry?"

Alicia understood this question and instead of showing how much she yearned for the coveted banana, she told her that she wasn't hungry at all. She might have added that her hunger had been sated by the washing of dishes. Seeing that Alicia had learned her first Christian lesson, the thin woman offered her the banana like alms given to the poor, which required gratitude beyond compare if Alicia was ever to see food again.

"Thank you very much. Thank you and your family very much."

"My family had nothing to do with this banana. Alicia, you must learn to thank those that rightly deserve it."

"Thank you for the banana, Mrs. Reed."

"You can eat it now."

"I will eat it later."

"Then you mustn't be hungry."

"I will eat it now."

Alicia ate the banana slowly and carefully, swallowing each bite noiselessly and smiling in appreciation of the food the Lord had provided for mankind on Earth. The thin woman seemed to rejoice, but Alicia was at a loss as to the source of her joy. Her eyes seemed to cut to her heart. Alicia would have to be careful with her choice of limited vocabulary.

That night Teresa took her to the shack out back where Alicia would have to share the space Teresa had considered her own. There was only one bunk. That was Teresa's. Not to make Alicia completely unwelcome, Teresa threw her a blanket that smelled of wet dog and garlic and told her to use the floor. Not being in her own house, Alicia obliged and lay her weary body on the blanket. The day had been long and her mind, jaws, and tongue were feeling the pressure of strange new words. Her tongue felt like a tired fish adapting to new waters.

As she was about to close her eyes and recapture what she had experienced that day, Alicia's thoughts were interrupted by Teresa's voice that latched on to her heart like a leech. She warned Alicia of the thin woman's meanness. She told her that the woman disliked thievery of any kind and that she had had a former servant girl arrested for eating a cherry that wasn't hers. The poor girl was hanged. The thin woman was responsible for the drought across the river and the gods would one day avenge her people. She told Alicia to keep her mouth shut and to keep away from the thin woman's son if she didn't want to end up pregnant with a strange child. María, the one that drowned herself, had been pregnant with his child.

S. Lecomte

Alicia didn't know what to believe, especially when the words spoken were in her own language.

-5-

My House Is Not Your House

Every morning began with the thin woman ringing the air against a rusty rail that hung like a rooster too dead to crow. The calm air would become agitated, and the thin woman would yell Teresa's and Alicia's names, shredding vowels with her razor-sharp tongue. Teresa was always first to get up. She would quickly get dressed, and like a duck without wings fly towards the thin woman to appear in the dim light before Alicia. Teresa would wait until Alicia caught up with her at the door. The thin woman would wrinkle her face, shake her body like a dog that's just been in the water, and say, "Teresa's an example you ought to follow, Alicia."

Alicia followed quietly in Teresa's footsteps and waited for the thin woman to give her orders. Although they were the same every morning, the thin woman didn't like anyone to anticipate her words. Words, after all, were sacred to a woman who began the morning with the Scriptures. Before Alicia and Teresa could touch any of the food laid out in the kitchen, the thin woman would read not just one prayer to get the wheels of the day spinning to a right start. No, she would read half a dozen pages of religious verses to make sure "her girls" got the correct message about life here on earth.

Although Alicia's mind couldn't comprehend the ancient English she heard bounce out of the thin woman's mouth, she understood the verses that dealt with God's anger, usually delivered because people didn't obey His rules. Alicia liked the sound of the thin woman's readings and smiled because she couldn't believe in God's anger. How could He be so mad all the time? Especially when He had had such a fine mother who had loved Him so much as a child. And didn't she cry tears so heavy that they shook the earth when they fell from her eyes as she witnessed His death on the cross? A boy who is loved doesn't become angry, Alicia thought. Perhaps the old English people needed such an angry God because they were not loving. And maybe the Bible she had read as a child had evolved in a different line.

After the Bible reading, Alicia said nothing until she was addressed. She had made the mistake of praising the thin woman's voice and reading only to be rebuked: "Reading the Bible isn't supposed to be a pleasure. It is our duty, Alicia. Remember that!"

Alicia would then go about her ordered chores. She fed the dogs, chickens, and sheep out back, but didn't stay long with them. She caressed the goats and sheep in passing and quickly returned to the kitchen where she was told to wash her hands by Teresa, only to be rebuked by the thin woman for wasting water.

Then Alicia and Teresa would begin the daily chore of making bologna sandwiches without cheese or lettuce. Just two pieces of bread, one slice of bologna and a small dab of mayonnaise spread as evenly as possible to give the bread taste. They slapped bread and meat together to feed the orchard hands who were waiting for their breakfast, lunch, and supper, each of these meals consisting of one bologna sandwich per person.

At first the thin woman had watched her like a hawk, but now that Alicia knew how to make a bologna sandwich, she could leave her alone and out of sight for a few minutes. Teresa took advantage of the thin woman's absence and raided the refrigerator like a rat, eating pieces of cheese, leftover roast, chunks of apple, and melon, her lips glowing with blood, fat, and fruit juices. Alicia might have done the same since she was quite hungry, but having been taught by her mother not to take what wasn't hers, she refused to act like a ferret, stealing what didn't belong to her.

Alicia, who was not intimidated by Teresa's lips that curled at the edges like lizard's tails, would admonish Teresa for stealing food. Teresa, however, continued to eat as if there were no tomorrow and called Alicia a stupid puta (whore) who fell from the moon. She could starve if she wanted. That was her business.

"But don't tell me when I'm supposed to eat. This old woman will kill us if we don't steal from her. You will starve, and she will say a prayer for you over your grave, Alicia! Wake up! You came from across the river!? What did you learn there?"

"I learned that honesty is the best policy."

"Where did you hear that?"

"On the tapes I studied."

"Tapes made on this side of the river! They want you to think the way they do, Alicia. Eat while you can! Take what you need. No one will help you in this world if you don't help yourself."

"Teresa, thank you for the advice, but I'm Alicia, not you."

"Then starve!"

The obese man would then appear in the kitchen, wheeling himself about like an armadillo in search of a place in the sand. He seemed to walk with his eyes closed until he had a cup or two of coffee to wake up his mind. Alicia would continue making bologna sandwiches while Teresa would fix the obese man's favorite breakfast, which came out of a box of cereal into a bowl. Teresa would pour the contents, throw some sugar, and cut up a banana or peach on top of it. She splashed milk all over and spooned some into his mouth. The obese man would chew the spoonful like a mill grinding nuts into powder, his mouth open to the flies the thin woman cursed because their son hadn't yet fixed the screening on the door. Teresa would then hand the spoon to the obese man, and he would eat the cereal by himself using his own hand until he realized his bowl was empty and he would ask Teresa for a refill. She repeated her routine until the box of cereal was completely empty.

The obese man would sit and drink coffee without reading the papers, which never appeared in this house. The news was best if it came from the source. The thin woman would appear with several cardboard boxes for the sandwiches, and the obese man would start twanging words through his sinuses until they came out with today's news, which reminded the thin woman of yesterday's news. Although she expressed her dislike for gossip, especially old, stale gossip, which she herself wouldn't have served up to any ear unless it was fresh out of somebody's mouth, she listened to the obese man's stories: Austin was messin' 'roun with a young heifer and had gotten the clap bad. So bad the doctors think he might have to have his penis circumnavigated the way the Jews done them. And the gal's bin through more 'an a dozen studs like him. Two of the fellers' penises and testicles done fell off of them. As bad as the pigs we castrated last year.

The thin woman would blush for propriety's sake and tell the obese man to hush up. The man, however, was hard to stop once his mouth had been put into motion, and the more he drank coffee the more he talked. During breakfast he would sometimes speak to himself for an hour while the thin woman was absent from his sight. But Alicia knew that men who claimed to be blind were quite aware of those present around them. The obese man never addressed her. He only spoke to himself even when he was speaking to the thin woman.

While the obese man was dissecting men and women and eating women's breasts as if they were a delicacy, the thin woman would be yelling for their son to get up and seize the worm like an early bird. He would always answer the same: "I'm no bird, and I hate worms."

Eventually he would make his appearance in the kitchen as the sun began to rise. He would then order Teresa to fix him some cereal. Teresa's eyes seemed to burn like hot coals. Alicia would have hated to be close to her at that moment. She thought that hell would break loose at any minute. Teresa moved quickly to the son's side, shook the empty cereal box, poured no milk and threw the banana peels on the table. Then she returned to the bologna sandwiches that kept piling up. Alicia wrapped, expecting the son to rise out of his chair and strangle Teresa for her arrogant behavior.

Alicia closed her eyes, but instead of awakening to the bloody scene of murder in the kitchen, she heard the young man berate his father for eating his favorite cereal.

"You always eat my cereal! No wonder you get fatter every day!"

"Mind yer mouth, boy. Or I'll leave ye high and dry as a riverbed when I die!"

The thin woman, hearing the commotion, took the obese man's side as usual and rebuked their son for not showing the proper respect due his father. Then she would touch her son's hair, whisper something in his ear, and he would order Teresa to fix him some flapjacks. Teresa would throw some flour into a bowl and today forgot the baking powder and eggs. When she fried and served the flapjacks, the son tasted them and cried out, "This is the worst horseshit I ever et!"

The thin woman couldn't believe her ears. Not only did she not like commotion of any type in her kitchen, she hated all forms of obscenity coming from her husband's and son's or anyone's mouths even when it wasn't in her own kitchen. Alicia had always found these words colorful in her own language and was glad to hear such words because the tapes she had studied had omitted the language of everyday people. Although she didn't understand the direct translation of each obscenity, Teresa filled in the blanks with "culo (ass), mierda (shit), cojones (balls), pendejo (fool)" and many more.

The thin woman wanted her kitchen as clean as a newly paved highway, and she objected to the language her son had used in front of Teresa and Alicia. The son's mouth was as motorized as his father's, unable to put the brakes on once it was in motion.

"That bitch's trying to poison me!"

"That's enough, Kyle," the thin woman yelled.

"I tole ye a hunret times not to mess 'round wit calica when ye got silk at home, boy," the obese man said, putting sand on the coals.

"What's that riddle supposed to mean?" the thin woman asked.

"For one to know and ye not to put yer nose where it don't belong. Com'on, boy. We'll get us some real breakfast in town."

The obese man and his offspring went out on the porch to smoke their cigarettes because the woman of the house couldn't stand them smoking up her curtains, her hair, her clothes. Alicia liked the smell of tobacco on a man. She thought the

thin woman was sick of men in general. Alicia and Teresa
loaded the pickup truck with boxes full of sandwiches that
were to be delivered to the orchards.

Before Alicia and Teresa left the kitchen for the orchards,
where they usually passed out the bologna sandwiches, the
thin woman offered them oranges or apples and two slices of
bread without butter or jam, which she claimed were detri-
mental to anyone's health. Teresa, who had stuffed herself earlier, wasn't hungry at all. The thin woman praised her for her
diligent work and wondered aloud how she could work so
much on almost no food at all. Alicia knew better but kept her
mouth shut. When the thin woman offered her the same
breakfast, she stuck her hand out for a second. The thin
woman's sharp eyes sliced her fingers with her look. Alicia
quickly changed her mind and said she wasn't hungry either.
The thin woman told them to get into the back of the truck.

They usually rode to the orchards along groves of orange
trees. Alicia could feel the cool morning air moist against her
face. The air out here was sweet and freer than in the house
where the watchful eye of the thin woman was everywhere.
Teresa, meanwhile, was eating a bologna sandwich. The first
few days Alicia hadn't touched the bread, meat and mayonnaise that didn't belong to her. Teresa thought Alicia had truly
come from either a strange planet or a village where the people had no brains. How could she feel she would be stealing
when the thin woman was working her to nothing but skin
and bones? On the fifth day, Alicia's stomach got the better of
her, and it received the bologna sandwich gratefully even if
Alicia still thought that taking things that didn't belong to her
was wrong. Then after that it got easier, and her stomach was
no longer grateful but accustomed to the bologna and bread.
By the end of the week it got so used to it that it demanded a
dietary change. Alicia, too, began taking bites of melon,

cheese, ham, and anything her stomach craved, all unnoticed by the thin woman, whose eyes were actually developing cataracts.

The ride ended at a campsite at the edge of the orchards. It looked like a country fair Alicia had once seen outside her village. The area was full of old cars and trucks with tents and awnings. When the pickup truck with its daily boxes of bologna sandwiches arrived, swarthy faces emerged into the morning light like large orderly ants lining up to receive their usual three bologna sandwiches. Alicia handed them out to the men who took them without thanks. Teresa handed them to the women who seemed less subdued and were more vociferous. The children waited in the background like sparrows in their nests for their mothers and fathers to return with the much-needed food. The line moved quickly and quietly.

Then the obese man would stand in the back of the pickup and read a list of names. At first Alicia had thought the lucky people might have won a prize, which might have consisted of bags of groceries so that their children could taste something other than bologna sandwiches. As the list was being read the next day, she realized that these people must have been related to Teresa because they also ate oranges, apples, and other fruit that belonged to the obese man. This fact didn't please the man or the son or especially the thin woman, and they had taken measures years ago to teach "these people" a lesson that their Catholic pastor had failed to do. "Ye know how dem Cat'lics are," the obese man would joke with Mr. Austin, the man with the unshaven buzzard face.

As the names were read off, the men, never the women, would step forward with their heads hanging down so low they looked like watermelons ready to fall off their branches if they could have grown in trees. Shame and remorse were not registered on their faces and this offended the obese man. All he could see was anger and rebellion. And it had to be quelled before these "locusts" ate his entire fields and orchards. The men, Alicia found out from Teresa later, were being punished for stealing the fruit of their own labor, which belonged to the obese man. Alicia didn't think that men should be punished for taking what was the fruit of their own labor. She thought they should be given more than bologna sandwiches. One day too early during her stay she mentioned that cheese would be a welcome change in addition to the bologna or ham or turkey, some fruit and candy, which she herself had tasted perhaps three or four times now. When the thin woman heard this "nonsense" coming from Alicia's mouth, she castigated her for thinking such stupid non-Christian thoughts. Of course, she repeated her famous phrase, "He who does not work does not eat!" Alicia might have argued that point, but no sooner had the thin woman heard Alicia's statement than she was sent to the chicken coop to scoop manure alongside the men who had stolen the fruit not of their land.

The men missed several days of work and were not paid the meager five cents a bushel since they had already eaten their fill. The men were lined up like prisoners taken during the orange-apple war and shipped on foot to various parts of the ranch to pick up horse manure, cattle dung, dog excrement, chicken shit and to empty the fecal matter that the obese man, his son and the thin woman had dumped into the septic system.

After all the waste was collected into a large pit, it was covered with plastic to see if gas would create a large balloon. Under the sun the waste boiled and digested itself once more until the balloon grew. The obese man had read about "shit makin' good sense" and thought the gas produced and sold in the U.S. would make him a fortune, until the balloon blew up and shook the world. The obese man vowed to find the guilty "murderer" of his balloon. But since there was plenty of manure he started all over and pretty soon a new balloon rose in the air.

One day, as the obese man allowed his son to read the list of those condemned to look for animal turds which had been overlooked in the wild pastures, a tall swarthy young man stepped forward. At first he said nothing and just listened. His brown eyes seemed intense, his dark brows knitted in anger. His full mouth was twisted with seriousness. It seemed as if the young man, who was a Comanche as Alicia found out later, was about to explode because of the injustices being carried out. Alicia and Teresa remained in the back of the pick-up, expecting the air to burst with blood, the blood of the obese man and his son, the blood of stolen oranges and stolen apples. But the young man was apparently polite and let the obese man's son read the entire list. Then nothing happened.

Alicia dreamed of the young man whose heroic deeds would soon come to bloom beneath the many trees. In her dream he sat among the people telling them that the land should belong to them as long as they worked it. Alicia didn't speak to him or make love to him.

The next day, however, she made the bologna sandwiches more quickly than usual and refused the bites of cheese and sausage that Teresa proffered like the refrigerator goddess she wanted to become.

After the usual list was read, Alicia saw the men not stepping forward. The obese man, who had not looked up until his list was complete, couldn't believe his eyes when he saw no one standing before him. His small eyes, swimming in his cheeks, looked like two ferocious fish through glass that protected on-lookers. He shook his body madly and spoke of "these people's" ungratefulness and thieving ways. He told them how wonderful his wife had been to them just making these wonderful bologna sandwiches.

"If they're so wonderful, why don't you eat them yourself?" a voice emerged out of the crowd. There was a breeze of laughter that made the leaves flutter. Then it died when the obese man asked for the voice to assume human form. Alicia, although she had never heard the voice that sounded very much like the man's on the tapes, knew the voice belonged to the young man who had in all probability inspired this morning's rebellion. The young man was wearing a red shirt and couldn't have been overlooked because of the energy that came from him as he stood in one spot, his feet planted in the ground like roots that demanded nutrients rightly theirs.

"We don't want your bologna sandwiches."

Everyone agreed.

"We want to get paid in money. We can make our own sandwiches with our own hands. And besides, nobody likes bologna here. We're sick of bologna!"

"And who de hell might ye be, boy? I don't recall hirin' yer ass!"

"My ass you didn't hire. I'm here to pick oranges."

"Boy, you've got a long ways to go. You ain't from 'rount here, are ye?"

"I'm from here alright, and I shore can talk lack y'all, but I got my law degree from Yale. Ain't that a kick in your pants. Yer papy'd never athought a dumb Comanche could ever have learned how to read! Well, here I am!"

"And yer fired! Git off my land or my boy here'll blow yer ass out for ye."

The young man raised his hands up in the air as the obese man's son cocked his rifle and pointed it at the young man's heart. Alicia was about to open her mouth in order to beg the obese man to spare his life when the young man disappeared into the morning light or lack of it, sparing her the embarrassment she might have felt afterwards.

With the young man gone, the men whose names had
been read off lined up and were taken to various parts of the
wilderness to pick up wild burro shit to replenish the obese
man's pit that was supposed to make him self-sufficient in gas.
Of course, his friend, the unshaven buzzard, laughed when he
heard the obese man say that. The chile the obese man was
fond of made enough gas in his stomach to supply all of Texas.

"All ye half to do is stick a pipe up yer ass, Ace, and dem
Arab's be outa bus'ness no time 't all."

"But then it might 'sphiziate dem all."

"Arabs ain't Christians nohow, Ace."

"Dat's true. Dat's true."

The night after the young man was fired, Alicia sat in the
dark listening to the buzzard and the obese man speak. The
obese man told him what had happened that morning and
expressed his "downright anger" at being accused of "spoilta-
tion" a word "downright" despised 'cause it was used by dem
communists who bin 'filtratin' this country lack day-old coffee grounds!"

"In de olten days we could whip 'em good! People knew
dere worth in gold, and dey worked without complainin'. I
don't whip 'em. No, Sir, we give 'em bologna sandwiches and
fresh spring water. And once a year we give 'em a fiesta with
the trimmin's. Ye bin to our fiestas, ye half."

"Could use more meat in de chile, Ace."

"I'll half to talk to Mae 'bout dat. So whadye find out
'bout dat Injun!?"

"His name's John O'Hara, but he now goes by the name
of Runnin' Antelope."

"Dem Injuns ain't never satisfied. We made 'em into honest Christians and see what dis one's done. Heathens is what
dey are. Reverting back to heathen ways, Austin."

"He's got his law degree from Yale."

"So what?"

"He's smarter dan his pappy."

"And who de hell was his pappy?"

"Black Elk, the one ye got to sign his land over to ye when he was drunk."

"A man shouldn't ought to drink while talkin' bus'ness, Austin."

"I reckon not, at least no wit ye."

"Let's talk 'bout dat new lady friend o' yers."

"I thought ye'd never ask."

That night Alicia dreamt that young man had vanished as a hawk into the night. She could feel his presence across the river, his eyes glowing with anger. All he had to do was throw a feather on the ground and he would revert back to human form. She knew in her heart he would come back.

-6-
Taken For a Ride

The obese man and the thin woman, being church-going folks, didn't allow the farmhands to work or think of working on Sunday, not even those who needed to eat. They would get up in the early morning hours, and Teresa would fry the obese man his usual Sunday bacon, sausage, and eggs, and several slices of cured Virginia ham which reminded him of days when he was a boy. The thin woman, aroused by the fat and the meat in the sizzling skillet, would rage up and down the hallway like an ascetic bent on starving one day out of the week for the Lord and taking the rest of the world down with her. With Bible in hand, she would rush into the kitchen and dash out of it, leaving some piece of the Scriptures dangling in midair. The words caught fire but were quickly extinguished by the obese man's chewing of ham, toast, cracklin's, sausage, jam, coffee and more of the same until he was in a sweat, his face red as a hot potbelly stove, his body exhausted from all the eating he had done.

The thin woman was definitely riled, and there was no letting up. When her son, whose name was Kyle, came down she reminded him that today was Sunday, and that he was, like a good Christian, supposed to fast for the Lord. The son, however, had given up such notions after he outgrew his boyhood and his mother's teat. The milk that had once graced the lining of his stomach had grown sour long ago. What good was a boy to be if he took up after his mother? No, he was his father's son. And Alicia would fix the same breakfast for the son because the obese man wasn't in the habit of wasting what was put before him. The thin woman yelled at her husband for ruining her son and pitting him against her. She resented their sniggering as she pointed to the Bible. The son ate everything Alicia put before him.

Even though the grease melted her taste buds, Alicia couldn't touch any of the food. She seemed to resist temptation. She and Teresa never got to sneak into the refrigerator on Sunday because the thin woman would read her Bible in the kitchen, her favorite place. Alicia thought that the woman's body existed on aromas alone, but that theory was quickly dashed out the window one day as she saw the thin woman devour a whole chicken by herself.

Alicia then remembered a nun who had once lived in her village. The woman was very beautiful and saintly, so saintly that she left the church because that was no life for her. Several months later one of the men saw her in a house where women sell their bodies. Could her sister be doing the same?

The thin woman pointed out Alicia's religious behavior because she too was getting thin and was beginning to grow pale. The son said, "She looks like she needs fattenin' up, Ma!"

"Kyle, wash your mouth out with soap," the thin woman said, perhaps thinking that her son wanted to get Alicia pregnant.

After satisfying their bellies, the men had their smoke on the porch and sat around until the thin woman told everyone to get in the pickup that would take them to the First Baptist Church. Alicia and Teresa sat in the back, taking in the fresh morning air as sustenance. At least, they had drunk several glasses of water, and Alicia had eaten bread she had stolen and saved for several days.

"Do you still know who you are?" Alicia asked.

"Yes . . . Teresa."

"I have a feeling that this woman is trying to make us into her."

"Don't worry so much! Do you see her fat husband? Well, what do you see?"

"A fat man!"

"Not just a fat man . . . a man who hasn't changed since she married him."

Teresa took the ride as if she were going to the fair, while Alicia wondered about her mother and Rosario. She tried to close her eyes to see what they looked like, but the harder she squeezed to get a recollection, the fuzzier their faces got. The boys from across the river had warned her. She would eventually forget her name, and her soul would wash downriver. Her mother must be walking to the village well with Rosario. If only she could find her sister! Alicia missed her family, but she had come with a mission to find a rich man who would change her life and the course of history in her village. Everyone, she thought, was depending on her, waiting for her to return with the man of their dreams, when in actuality they were getting drunk, yelling at each other, especially at the children who went out to throw rocks at mangy dogs and so on. Some, perhaps, already thought she had died in the desert and never made it to the river.

When they reached the church, the obese man and his son suddenly turned into sheep as they shook the pastor's hand. The thin woman followed her husband's lead, and they all sat up front to be closer to the pulpit so that God could have a closer look at them and vice-versa. Alicia and Teresa stood in the back and watched the people sing their hearts out. The pastor then got on his pulpit and yelled words that Alicia had never understood. All she knew was that the preacher looked and seemed angry as he shook his fist at the people. She also understood that the obese man and his son might go to Hell with all those Sunday meat-eating men as the preacher's fingering omitted no one. The preacher's face turned watermelon red as he yelled for all ears to hear. The walls and windows shook as if God Himself were trying to bring down the house, perhaps to rebuild it. Then the plate was passed and the obese man took out a handful of bills and threw them on the plate, while everyone else placed an envelope on it, sealed for no eyes to see.

The plate wended its way like a snake through the aisles, its golden eyes filling up with money. When the plate reached Alicia, she passed it to Teresa, and she passed it on. Since Alicia had no money and was paid in room and board, she couldn't very well put the money she wasn't getting in a plate already too full. The pastor then received the plate, raised it to the ceiling and thanked God for his bountiful mercies. Before anyone left the church, however, he said a few words to those standing in the back.

"Even a single penny from your meager pockets would make the Lord happy!"

They all sang a song and everyone smiled, happy to be leaving the confines of the walls, happy souls free to go to lunch and picnics, except for the thin woman who believed in old-fashioned ways that were bound to make the Lord worthy of her and her worthy of the Lord.

The obese man and his son wanted to go out to lunch and treat Teresa and Alicia to the famous chile burger with all the trimmings, but the thin woman, apparently worn out by the Scriptures she so often quoted to no avail, had other plans. She mentioned string beans to be snapped, bedding to be washed and other innumerable chores that couldn't wait. The obese man reminded his wife of the religious custom of resting on Sundays because the Lord Himself had taken the day off to have a beer and a smoke. This explanation got the thin woman's feathers ruffled.

"God didn't drink! And He surely didn't smoke!"

"So why did He make tobacco!?"

"It evolved, but He didn't create it. It was scientists with faulty brains that grew such weed."

"Woman, I know they had beer in Heaven or they wouldn't have sold so much wine!"

The philosophical argument ended at the ranch, and the women would be let off to work. The obese man and his son would drive off and not come home until evening. When they did come back (sometimes they stayed in town), they would both yell out the thin woman's name. And she would come down in her nightgown, shotgun in hand, threatening to shoot all the air out of the obese man's belly for being too drunk to move. Instead of walking in on their own, they would lie in the dirt a while and then the thin woman would rouse Alicia and Teresa out of bed to drag her husband and son into the house.

One Sunday afternoon while Alicia was cleaning out chicken shit from the chicken coop, because she had expressed the wish not to go to church because she had her own views of God to Teresa, who in turn related this to the thin woman, the son came out to see her. He approached like a fox ready to steal eggs that were not his. Alicia, not knowing his intentions, continued to shovel chicken shit into the wheelbarrow before her and tried to ignore his unwelcome presence. She would rather have been left alone with the punishment but without the insults she thought were about to flog her mind. His presence made her feel awkward as he seemed to stare at her ankles and calves. Alicia walked in the chicken shit barefoot, not wanting to ruin the only pair of shoes she had worn for years.

"I ain't like them," he said in a gentle and sympathetic voice. Alicia, who was keen on accents since she had begun her real study of English, suddenly realized that the son had lost his father's tone of voice and twanging in his nose. His voice sounded like his mother's. Could she expect the same words, the same dryness, the same caustic remarks that at first didn't burn through her skin but now did?

"You look very beautiful, even shoveling that manure, Alicia. I have admired you from afar and I think you deserve better than what you're getting here. If you marry me, you can eat all the oranges you want. I mean, you can have anything at all: bacon, sausage, cereal, anything. I just hate to see you eating bologna sandwiches. So how about it?"

Alicia let his words dangle in midair, wanting him to think about the meaning of his words. Words to Alicia had become everything, especially those in English, which could either prevent her from being punished by the thin woman from absurdities committed in the name of grammar or lack of it or prevent her from being herself.

Alicia scooped up a shovel full and for some unknown reason had a desire to throw the chicken shit in the son's face to see how he would react. He had said that he wasn't like his parents and she wanted proof of it. She threw the chicken shit into the wheelbarrow instead. She wondered why this wolf had come in sheep's clothing. Why had he changed his tune? She knew for a fact that he had taken Teresa out for weeks or months before her arrival and that he no longer wanted her. Teresa had boasted of his long penis and his male prowess before he dumped her. Lucky she was still on the ranch premises. Teresa had mentioned that she wasn't going to be a servant long and that Kyle would see that she was the woman for him. Teresa had been robbed of a wedding, of a husband, of a ranch, of all the oranges she could eat and she was out to get even with Kyle. Alicia was aware of it all.

"How about it?"

"Bologna sandwiches are fine."

"That's not what I asked!" he said, his voice changing already.

"What did you ask?"

"Will you marry me? Alicia, my heart aches for you! I dream of you at night. I'm losing my appetite."

Alicia had seen him sleep and eat as if there were no tomorrow and couldn't believe that he had lost sleep or food over her.

"You look healthy to me. Now, please, go away before your mother sees you talking to me. I can't marry you just like that. I must know the person to be a good person."

"I am a good person!"

"Then join me in cleaning this manure."

Kyle's face didn't express the distasteful look she had expected. Instead, his lips bloomed a wonderfully happy smile. He jumped into the chicken shit like a hog entering Heaven, grabbed a shovel, and like a man in love, scooped up every drop of chicken shit before Alicia could even say another word.

Alicia wasn't at all surprised to see a man like Kyle clean all the chicken shit as if he had been created on earth for that sole purpose. She recalled men back in her village who had starved to death out of love. Some had killed because of love. Some had robbed. Others had left the village out of shame. So, cleaning chicken shit really proved nothing to Alicia since she was, after all, doing it herself. And just because she was cleaning chicken shit out of the coops didn't especially mean that she was in love with Kyle, who was cleaning it because he thought he was in love with the most beautiful girl on earth, as he had been with Teresa and others.

As soon as the chicken shit was carted away into the garden where the thin woman had a compost pit, Kyle told Alicia that he felt more in love now than he ever did in his life. Now that he had sacrificed whatever he was supposed to have sacrificed, he almost demanded that she now go with him for a ride downtown, take in a movie and a hamburger.

Kyle's shirt and pants were covered with sweat and chicken shit. His smile, stupid and childish, made him look innocent. Alicia, who had heard of but never eaten a hamburger, decided to go and see the town that had so far existed out of her reach. She agreed to go with him. Kyle, like a colt just foaled, ran to change his clothes, his legs causing him to fall under the sudden surprise Alicia had given him as if she had thrown a bone to a starving pup.

Lucky for Alicia, the thin woman had taken Teresa into town to visit an old friend to whom she always took a basket of oranges every Sunday. Alicia might have otherwise caught her wrath, and Kyle would have been castigated for going out with one not his own kind, but there she stood in her only dress, clean and ready to taste the great American burger that had become a symbol all over the world, unbeknownst to Alicia. She knew, however, that it was made with pure beef ground into a paste, barbecued, put between two round pieces of bread, with pieces of lettuce, tomatoes, onions, catsup, pickles, mayonnaise. She remembered the wonderful colored picture of one such hamburger she had cut out of a magazine left by a wandering tourist. Alicia had been thirteen when she came to know the meaning of this hamburger that hung yellowing on her walls until it fell to dust. She dreamed that one day she would eat such a hamburger, and here right now she saw her dream realizing itself before her very eyes. She was so lucky!

Kyle drove his small red car around, jumped out, opened the door and led Alicia down the stairs as if she were a princess. Alicia enjoyed the ride down the highway with its sparse shrubs and cactus. Outside the chicken shit, Kyle seemed quiet. Alicia didn't want to disturb her own solitude by asking questions. All she wanted was a hamburger with all the trimmings and nothing more. All he wanted was a wife. The music from the radio played on. The song seemed sad to Alicia, although she didn't understand why Kyle was crying just because of a song. He snorted his nose, tears streaming down his cheeks like an overflowing well. She touched his tears to see if they were real, and he smiled like a burro just because of a woman's touch. Alicia quickly withdrew her hand and said she was sorry she had touched his cheek. It was all right with him. She could touch "anythang she was wantin' to!"

Alicia noticed a change in his words and tone of voice. Had the car transformed his soul? He now sounded like his father, and the sight of the obese man in her mind made her move away from him.

"When ye're my wife, I 'spect ye'll want new clothes, honey! I'll treat ye like a queen. Ye'll half everythang, anythang you want. I cain't wait for us to be walkin' down that aisle. Ye'll make me so happy. I cain't wait for my Pappy to hear the news!"

Alicia was being carried away by this man she hardly knew. It is true, her mother had sent her across the river in search of a rich man to save her family and village from starvation and death, and Kyle would inherit the orchards and his father's business. Alicia, however, had read several romance novels as a young girl and even though the translations had been expunged by a censor suffering from glaucoma, the text did not omit the fact that love was more than cleaning chicken shit and buying her a hamburger. The women in the books she had read may have swooned over their lovers, but it was out of love and because of their free will. Alicia may have confused love and free will, but she was on the right track. She had to have a voice in this. She had an opinion to express and express it she did!

Alicia opened her mouth and without hesitation said, "You didn't ask me if I wanted to get married! Is it not proper for the people here to court? Is that the word? To court?"

Kyle, of course, agreed to court, to woo her with gifts, and poetry and songs, if need be. He had taken up the guitar when he was twelve but had given up on the idea of becoming a country-western singer after the second or third lesson. His fingers had gotten cut up on the guitar strings and he just wasn't cut out to be a singer.

Alicia let him ramble, hoping he would tire of her as quickly as he had of Teresa and the others who had lost more than their virginity to this young insatiable buck. Alicia was aware of his sexual prowess, but she couldn't give in to a man with who she wasn't in love, not even if he promised her all the oranges grown in the world, which had already been given to Teresa and the others.

Kyle ordered the largest and juiciest hamburger with all the trimmings Alicia had wanted. When she took the first bite, she felt as if she had suddenly risen to Heaven, but Kyle was staring at her like a vulture whose eyes devoured each bite she was taking. He asked her how the hamburger tasted. She stopped eating and said that it was the best meal she had had since she had crossed the river.

After her stomach felt the delight that food could bring to the human soul, she licked her lips like a kitten and Kyle ran off and bought what he called "the piss de resistants" which was French for a strawberry milkshake, his favorite, which he thought would become hers too once they were wed. Alicia drank the milkshake, catching her breath here and there like a wild cat drinking at the river after too long a time in the desert. She was stuffed and feeling sick, but Kyle wanted her

to taste of the fruits of delight denied in her childhood. He
wanted to take her out for pizza right after that to prove how
much he truly loved her. After all, how else could he prove his
love in an age where chivalry was truly dead?

Alicia could eat no more, and Kyle looked disappointed
and deprived of his opportunity to show her what he was
made of. Alicia wanted to be taken back home to rest her
stomach, which had now found out what sin really was. Kyle
drove towards the groves and stopped the car near the river.
The sun was setting above the buttes and he told her how
much he wanted to sit with her on his porch once they got
married.

Alicia was getting sick, not only of hearing how he wanted to get married. As he leaned over to kiss her on the lips,
Alicia threw up milkshake, lettuce, mayonnaise, pickles, and
hamburger right in Kyle's face. That was payment for the
hamburger that was to buy him a kiss and a ride on the heifer
he had to try out as he had the others just before he "married"
them.

That was to be their first and last date. Alicia had had a
premonition that men don't buy women hamburgers without
wanting payment in return. And Alicia wasn't about to pay
with her virginity. She was worth more, much more than all
the orange orchards that came without love.

-7-
Among the People

After his first date, which Kyle thought was the beginning of a beautiful relationship, he tried to take her to a Chinese restaurant that had opened in this part of the world to give the inhabitants a taste of the Orient. Alicia had a clear recollection of the hamburger incident and refused to go with him, but Kyle was not a man to be defeated by a woman, especially when he was almost engaged and married at the same time.

Having watched far too many westerns with his favorite hero—The Duke—and having heard so many western love songs that dealt more with horses and doggies than women, Kyle knew that if he persisted, the woman would give in. After all, the others had. This stubbornness on the part of Alicia made her more appealing.

Kyle came at her with a volley of things to eat. He knew that the way to these women's hearts was through their stomachs. He shoved steaks, fries, chile, chicken, fried snake, armadillo, deer, pork her way. She refused. He pelted fruit at her. She refused. What about an ice cream sundae? Although she didn't know what it looked or tasted like, Alicia refused out of frustration with this man who didn't seem to understand her English. But then José back in her village had not understood her Spanish. José had, of course, had a college education and studied in Madrid where he had perfected his Castilian accent and he now spoke Spanish with a lisp.

Kyle soon got the message that Alicia was not a woman bought for a bag of fries. This woman was wanting more than food. He tried picking his guitar to no avail. He had nothing to offer but himself. He wanted her. And because he wanted her, she must have wanted him too. This thought was as clear as a reflection of his face in the mirror.

Alicia told him that she wasn't hungry and that she was waiting for the right man to come along and that her refusal shouldn't be taken as a reflection on him. Kyle couldn't believe his ears even though she had repeated this message a hundred times. Alicia learned that men in love lost their minds and heard nothing but the beating of their own hearts. Kyle walked away hurt—cut down by a woman he had given his life to. He felt he had sacrificed not only six dollars and seventy-nine cents to feed her—that he could live with—but he had sacrificed his pride by shoveling chicken shit for a woman who had no real appreciation of the finer things in life—him!

Kyle walked away angry. While he was "courting" Alicia, Teresa, who was still "in love" with the little boss, was envious, jealous, and spitefully vengeful of her because she had been chosen above all the women in the orchard. Teresa had declared war and made sure to wound Alicia each day. Teresa took bites out of cheese, fruits, bread, and left her teeth marks as proof of Alicia's thieving ways. The thin woman, discovering these criminal activities, was utterly dismayed, taken aback. She suddenly slapped Alicia's face and then asked Teresa who had done such an uncivilized thing. Teresa told her that the teeth marks matched Alicia's. The thin woman again slapped Alicia's face to remind her of the first slap, which was supposed to remind her of her guilt.

When the thin woman asked Alicia to confess her crimes, Alicia denied having done anything, but didn't point the finger at Teresa whose lizard smile now adorned her mouth. The thin woman, being a church-going Christian, wasn't as thin on compassion as she might appear now. She told Alicia that she could stay on but that she would have to shovel more chicken shit. One might have thought that with Alicia cleaning out the coops, the chickens would have run out of shit, but as everyone knows, what is eaten must be excreted.

Teresa, whose blood didn't cease boiling even when the temperature fell in the evening, was out to get Alicia who was as defenseless as a lamb. Teresa stuck ants and spiders in the thin woman's bed and dirtied the bathroom with her own excrement and blamed it all on Alicia. The thin woman was more and more frustrated because of the lack of effect her punishment was having on Alicia.

Kyle, who felt he had been cruelly rejected, spread the rumor that he was getting married to Alicia anyway. When the news reached Teresa's ears, she rushed at Alicia, grabbed her by the throat and shook her until she almost lost consciousness. Teresa's eyes had grown as large as saucers and the anger and envy poured out in warm tears like molten lava that singed Alicia's face. Capable of murder, Teresa eventually let go of Alicia's throat, thinking perhaps that it was no different than the throats of chickens she had run through with the axe. Teresa had lopped off a thousand chicken heads like an executioner, unfeeling and without regard for chicken life.

Even though Teresa recognized Alicia as a human being, she would have liked for her to disappear or die. Alicia had heard Teresa pray for her death. She had even heard her speak of her death in her sleep. When Alicia recovered her breath, she asked her why she was so angry.

"You must be as thick in the head as the burros! You knew me and Kyle had a thing going!"

"But I have done nothing with him. I don't even like the man."

"So why are you marrying him?"

"He's marrying me, but I'm not marrying him."

"Same difference."

"I don't want to marry him."

"Still, he wants to marry you instead of me. You'll pay for this. To think, I took you under my wing like a sister. I fed you. I taught you how to be safe. And then you steal my husband!"

"I didn't know he was your husband."

"You stole the husband I could have had if you hadn't showed up and paraded your round ass before him like a mare in heat! I have eyes, you know!"

When morning came, Alicia was ready to leave as she had come so that Teresa could play her cards and regain the upper hand over Kyle. As she walked out of the shack, the thin woman and the sheriff were standing in her way. They asked her if she was planning to take a trip. Alicia knew nothing about any trip.

When they walked into the kitchen, she figured out that Teresa had committed another crime in her name and that she would have to pay for it, perhaps with her life. The thin woman disclosed that five hundred dollars had been stolen from her secret box and that Alicia must have been an accomplice to the robbery because she had shared the shack with Teresa and because "these people stick together." Alicia denied ever having stolen anything. The thin woman brought up the teeth marks on the cheese and pears, her favorite. The sheriff, a man with a kind face, even if he had been born in the same town as the thin woman, told the thin woman that he couldn't see arresting Alicia for a crime she didn't commit. The thin woman was furious because her logic had been questioned.

"Ma'am, I can't arrest dis beautiful girl."

80

S. Leeomte

"You said 'beautiful.'"

"I'm sorry. I can't arrest dis woman for a crime committed by another."

"Someone's got to be punished for the theft!"

"But not dis woman. Just think, Ma'am. Would dis woman have stuck 'round if she had done dat. I mean, usually the criminal leaves town."

"Sheriff, you must not watch television very much. The murderer always sticks around to kill another victim. And she will steal again."

"But Teresa's gone wit yer money!"

"It might as well be her doing!"

"Ma'am, we'll put out an APB on her, but I got me a feelin' she's done crossed the river by now."

When the sheriff left the premises, the thin woman forgot about the five hundred dollars Teresa had stolen from her and said, "You'll never marry my son. You stay away from him. Do you hear me?"

"I don't want to marry him. I never wanted to marry him."

"So now he's not good enough for you, is that it? Do you think you're better than us?"

Before Alicia could answer, the thin woman opened the door and pointed to it. Alicia understood that she was no longer wanted here.

"You wait outside! I am not what you think I am. I am not that cruel woman you all think I am. That's what you think and I know it. My church has not taught me to be evil to others. And to think evil of others is evil. We will keep you out in the orchards with your people. But we will keep an eye out on you, Alicia!"

Alicia walked out, and several hours later the obese man himself drove her to the orchards where she would be banished until the thin woman changed her mind. Unlike Teresa, she didn't seem to understand that freedom was right across

81

the river or down the road into town. But freedom also meant being without food. Fate and the grace of people, not unlike the thin woman's, would have to do for now.

The obese man told Alicia not to be upset with his wife and to imagine the life he had had with her for the last thirty-five years. The woman had sucked his dreams dry. She had killed the woman he had been in love with. Literally, of course. And his heart has been aching ever since. Some things never heal. He told her not to worry about the five hundred dollars Teresa had taken, but if she could marry Kyle, it would do his heart good to know that his son was in good hands. Think about it. Kyle really loved her. When they came to the edge of the orchards, the obese man pulled out his wallet and gave her several twenty-dollar bills, which she at first refused by pushing his hands away. Alicia had learned that nothing was really for nothing. What would the obese man want in return? He insisted, and like a sly snake his hand snuck the money into her bosom, and he laughed obesely leaving her to fend for herself. The truck drove off.

Alicia was left alone and in the dark, but free from the tyranny of the thin woman. No sooner had the truck left than she was surrounded by faces she thought were of her own kind. They were swarthy but unfriendly as they asked her what she wanted here. She told them in a language they understood that she had been brought to the orchards to pick oranges. A loud voice cried out that there were already too many ants on this anthill and that she would be better off picking spinach or cotton downriver. The harvest here would soon be over and they would have to be moving to greener pastures like locusts reaping everything in their way to feed themselves, to multiply their own kind and then to die of starvation in some corner of the field.

A short woman with hardly any teeth slithered out of the dark and told Alicia she would die here if she were to pick oranges. Alicia didn't know what she was trying to tell her. She told her the sun would bake her brains until she wouldn't know her name, until her belly ached for food and her tongue begged for drops of water. Her face, now beautiful and smooth as a glazed bun, would turn old and crack like dried clay, and no man would find her attractive. And if she married one of the field hands, he would have to get drunk and beat her because she would be too ugly to be mounted. And God would look down and laugh Himself to sleep. The toothless woman didn't believe in God, only in death, and even though Alicia had not gone to church much, she was frightened by the idea of death without continuation of some sort of life. Alicia believed in a Heaven where wishes came true and in a Hell where evil people were put in a large room with others of their kind. The thin woman would be punished by herself.

The toothless woman advised her not to spend her first night here but to move on to the road where men roamed the desert in search of themselves. She would have better luck there. These lonely men had nothing but sand in their souls and were in need of women to tell them who they were. Desert men always need women to fill the void around them, but these men quickly tire of women once they've played with them and filled their void.

Alicia didn't want to roam the highway. Many other faces surrounded her. One among them cried out that she was the bologna girl. The face belonged to a young woman. She cried out that Alicia was one of their prosecutors, that she had made lousy bologna sandwiches, while she had eaten her fill like a kitten fed by its mistress's hand. The young woman spoke as loudly as possible to prove that she was being murdered by the lack of mayonnaise and rotten meat Alicia had fed her. Other voices quickly recognized Alicia for what she was. All the faces belonged to women of all ages, their eyes glowing with Teresa's envy and jealousy. They called her names she had heard used against evil women back in her village, and Alicia felt frightened for her life as she had witnessed a woman's death at the hands of women who had hatched out of vulture's eggs. These women claimed that she had fed them poisoned meat and that their children had been sick for weeks now. They accused her of having been the young master's bitch and that he had gotten tired of her because she was nothing but a thief. They wanted nothing to do with her, and to make sure she knew she wasn't wanted here, they threw rocks and oranges at her until she collapsed.

When she awoke in the early morning light, Alicia was lying down, not on the road or in the orchard or in Heaven as she had expected it, but in a tent. The face of a young girl hung above her like a colorful exotic butterfly, her hair braided with yellow, red, and blue clay beads. Her eyes reminded Alicia of a wild antelope's she had once seen come to the river at home. Alicia attempted to get up but the young girl told her to lie still as she placed a cold wet rag on her forehead. Alicia suddenly felt pain everywhere in her body and couldn't understand why people of her own kind had tried to kill her.

The young girl with antelope eyes vanished like an apparition and reappeared with aromas familiar to her. The young girl was holding a plate of frijoles and tortillas Alicia had not tasted since she had crossed the river. She sat down next to her and as soon as she tasted the first bite, Alicia choked on her own tears like a woman recognizing the error of her ways. Her mother's face suddenly appeared and replaced the young girl's.

"Alicia, are you all right, my daughter?"

"Yes, Mamá."

"What is the bruise on your head?"

"It's nothing, Mamá. Our own people were hungry, and they wanted to eat my body instead of the oranges and bologna sandwiches."

"What is a bologna sandwich, my daughter?"

"It is something our people hate, especially with no mayonnaise."

"What is mayonnaise?"

"It is something they put on bologna sandwiches."

"Alicia, I see you have learned a lot."

"Mamá, I want to come home."

"My poor Alicia, you must not despair. For a beautiful girl like you there are a thousand princes to choose from."

"One would be a miracle."

"Miracles will happen, Alicia, but like good wine, they too must ferment and come to life on their own time."

The young girl wiped the tears from Alicia's eyes and continued to feed her frijoles and pieces of tortilla, reassuring her that she would live. As soon as she was fed, Alicia's soul soared. The young girl vanished through the hole in the tent and an older woman with the same type of face and beaded braids knelt down beside her. Alicia wondered if she might not be in Heaven.

The older woman told her she was a long way from there. She covered her with a blanket and advised her not to pick oranges today.

"How did I get here?" she asked.

"My son found you unconscious in the orchards. My daughter and I are the only ones that pick oranges now. Men always open their mouths and either get beaten or killed."

The older woman's son had vowed to avenge his father's death and was organizing the peons into unions to bring the fruit and vegetable industries to their knees, to show them that they too should be humble to the sacred land and to the hands that cared for it. He demanded steady wages and enough food to feed the people. He demanded that children no longer be exploited, although the parents were the ones who forced their own children to perform such labor. He demanded that the ranch owners respect the peons as human beings. His father had been killed for demanding the same, by a bullet through the head. Her son, however, had a degree from Yale law school. That had made him a prisoner of himself.

Alicia understood the older woman's son was the young Indian man called Running Antelope, and her heart filled with pride for the young brave man who was to perform heroic deeds. The older woman's son only came at night because of the danger that might befall him. Alicia's heart suddenly felt strange as she thought of him, but waiting for him would accomplish nothing in her life. Even if it was love she felt for a stranger, he could never be rich, and her mother and the entire village would laugh at her for marrying an Indian instead of the millionaire who was to cure them of all their ills.

So far Alicia knew that rich men like Kyle and the obese man had no love in their hearts and that men with hearts had no money. This generalization left her cold, especially when she thought of the poor men and women who had stoned her because their hearts were too big!

- 8 -

Good Men Stand Alone

Instead of lying in self-pity for bruises inflicted by her own people, Alicia got up and joined the older woman, whose name was Yellow Rose and whose daughter was Pale Moon. Alicia came out on her own two feet and said she would show her own kind that she had every right to work in these orchards. The older woman said nothing as she walked to the main shed where baskets were lying around waiting to be filled. Alicia and Pale Moon followed in silence in Yellow Rose's footsteps. Then they began picking oranges like birds come to fill their bellies.

Yellow Rose and Pale Moon didn't eat the white man's bologna sandwiches because it wasn't food that came from the earth. Yellow Rose told Alicia later that the white man's food contained poisons that the gods had never heard of. Even the white man's Bible didn't have a list of them. Maybe it mentioned coffee, Coca-Cola and tea, but it didn't have the others. Mormons and Jehovah's Witnesses had apparently made their rounds here and told the Indians and Mexicans they would go to hell if they drank anything with caffeine. They were laughed out of the camp when someone with a smart mouth said that they all must be in Heaven since they couldn't afford coffee.

Alicia Maravilla

Yellow Rose told Alicia that people had to be careful when accepting from others. She pointed to Alicia's own people and said that the women gave of what they had as willingly as snakes giving away their venom and demanded twice in return. The men never gave. They took. It didn't matter what color they were, black, white, yellow or red. All men took.

Alicia picked oranges with the Indian women. There were no Indian men in the orchards, only Mexican men. Indian men, Yellow Rose told her later, were men whose hearts had been wounded by the bullets and long knives of history. The men were filled with pride and would rather starve to death than to work for the white man. White and Mexican men had no pride according to Yellow Rose. They cared too much for their bellies. White men had no principles. Their words were always empty and full of lies. The white man had changed his own God to fit his purposes. God must have had a hard time recognizing Himself when he shaved in the morning and put his suit on to go to work at His bank. "America is one giant bank and God must be locked up in a vault. The white man has clipped His wings, and He cannot return to Heaven. And if He did, Alicia, He wouldn't be able to breathe, the air being so bad up there."

The Indian women were a quiet lot, picking oranges with a silent cadence that appealed to Alicia. The Mexican men and women working on the other side of the orchards were loud and, at times, fights erupted among them. The baskets were filled and taken to a truck that then drove off with the oranges, leaving a trail of dust.

Pale Moon was no more than fifteen, but she was a woman who worked and earned her keep. Alicia was amazed at how quickly Pale Moon plucked the oranges out of the trees like a pickpocket. Pale Moon told Alicia that this kind of work was not for her and that one day she would go to the university as her brother had. Pale Moon wanted to study medicine and

S. Leeomte

become a doctor on a reservation. She didn't want to make a lot of money. All she wanted was a small house, a husband who respected himself and who would respect her, and a white horse that she would ride along the mountain trails. She dreamt of this white horse every night.

Pale Moon knew of this modern world, of its fast cars that ended nowhere, of its fast foods that killed people with heart attacks, of alcohol that poisoned livers, of fast women that infected men's brains.

"Men are so weak compared to women, Alicia. Women bear children, bear men's pains, and are beaten for it. Men can only hide behind the bottle and inside their women's wombs. They are such babies!"

Pale Moon was angry at all men, especially at her non-existent father, who had disappeared one day and drowned in a nearby pond because he couldn't find his way home. The police said that his blood had contained alcohol. Yellow Rose had never known her husband to drink, but she believed the story because her husband was a man like any man, who could break and swim in his own pity to recapture the pain and anger of being an Indian under white man's rules. Pale Moon couldn't forgive her father for having abandoned her.

Yellow Rose picked oranges like a bird of prey with several beaks, her hands quicker than a magician's. The oranges fell five by five into her basket like heads decapitated from the obese man's neck and men like him. The obese man and his son stuck around in their trucks, fond of watching modern-day slaves working in the Garden of Eden to make them happy. The obese man and his son had the music on—the kind of music Alicia finally understood. The songs dealt with men who got drunk and left their women or with men who drank because their women left them. The songs blamed the women for being evil. The songs had made Kyle want to marry Alicia. The obese man and his son sat in the truck, having beers and smokes.

Alicia could see anger fly out of Yellow Rose's eyes like hawks sent out to choke the obese man by the throat. Alicia knew how the obese man's father had stolen this land, the orchards, from Running Antelope's father. Of course, that was in the past, and the obese man, being white, had no real recollection of any wrongdoing. The obese man, whose memory was as short as he was nearsighted, couldn't see why "these people" couldn't forgive and forget as he did. It was during these deep moments that the obese man brought up his Christian feelings that were tied to flag and country. These people, he thought, ought to be grateful to be living in a country that prided itself on freedom and democracy.

The day Alicia began working in the orchards, the obese man gathered everyone except the Indians, who ate their own food without being compensated for it. The obese man stood in the back of the pickup, wiped the sweat from his forehead, and like an orator in love with his own voice, he declared that they would no longer have to eat bologna sandwiches. Voices of dissent rose from the crowd below him, even from those who had eaten bologna and hated it. Then the obese man raised his hands in the air like a false prophet trying to quell the storm he had created and cried out, "We've changed the menu!" He paused again to see a sea of swarthy faces with eyes that expressed great surprise and even greater fear of the unknown. Would they have to eat snake or rat sandwiches while he ate roast beef, barbecued ribs, and sausage? Then the obese man opened his mouth, like an executioner offering reprieve and said, "Salami, Italian salami sandwiches!" He expected to hear them cry out hurrahs as if he were a hero returning alive from battle. Instead, the crowd went wild and rebellious, demanding the old-time bologna.

S. Leconte

"No salami! No salami! No salami!"

Alicia, who had heard of salami through her lessons, but had never tasted it, yelled that salami was better than bologna. The crowd went wild against her and continued to yell no to salami. The obese man shook several sticks of salami in the air, and the crowd recognized them as something akin to sausage. Someone cried out that it had been years since she had eaten or smelled a piece of sausage. Everyone agreed that salami was better than bologna, even though they had yet to taste the salami. It looked and tasted better, even if it had yet to be tasted, because it was different. They looked at Alicia, especially the men, and thanked her for opening their taste buds to something new. The obese man told them that he was a fair man and a Democrat, who didn't like to impose his views and choices on other people. He would allow them to make up their own minds. His son sliced the salami sticks and everyone stepped up to the truck and partook of the communion, except the Indians and Alicia, who watched in the background.

Many of the women spat the salami out and cursed Alicia, the bologna girl, for opening her mouth. Lucky for her, there were no rocks at hand or they might have stoned her for suggesting a change in diet, which their husbands were eager to try. Most of the faces, who were tasting their third and even fourth piece of salami, thought it was better than bologna. The obese man was delighted by their choice. He apparently was getting this salami cheap, directly from Italy, and would save a fortune on the bologna, produced not in Bologna, Italy, but in St. Paul-Minneapolis. The orchard workers were divided. Most of the women liked the bologna; the men and some of the women wanted a change and opted for salami. The obese man told them all that this being a democratic country, they would have to choose. That day fifty-one percent were for salami; forty-nine for bologna. What's fair is fair! Everyone would have to eat salami sandwiches from now on even though thirty-five percent of the fifty-one percent got sick of the salami within several days. But there was no turning back. Once you voted for something, there was no pulling the lever back. Salami it was!

The Indian women and Alicia had gone back to picking oranges while the Mexican men and women argued about the choices available in life. Alicia's body, unused to such physical labor, grew tired, but she stuck to her basket like the rest of the women and was glad when the sun had begun to set. As she closed her eyes, all she could see was oranges. The entire universe was populated by oranges. She swore to herself that as long as she would live, she would not eat another orange, although she had craved them as a child.

The day done, Alicia followed Yellow Rose and Pale Moon, her arms and legs ready to fall off as she handed in her basket and received the five cents per bushel she had picked. The money felt strange in her hand since she had never had money. What could she do with this money? American dollars? When she reached Yellow Rose's tent, she handed her the money for the food and place in her tent, but Yellow Rose would not hear of it. She pushed Alicia's hand away and told her that she couldn't take money from one more needy than herself. And what would the world come to if you couldn't help another human being?

Pale Moon went out and gathered some firewood and returned without the oranges that most Mexican girls stole from the white man's trees to repay him for the salami sandwiches they were to eat from now on. Alicia helped Yellow Rose with the frijoles and tortillas.

The air was hot and dry, and the fire made it hotter, but the smell of oil and flour brought the image of her mother up from the deep recesses of her mind. Yellow Rose reminded her of her own mother. She was a mother who cared for her children. She resented most men because they were of bad faith. Ever since her husband had died, men, including Indians with white men's souls, had come around like flies smelling her for sex.

"Men only come around for sex. They want to infect women's bodies with their stupid weaknesses. Men ejaculate their sadness into women's vaginas and we give birth to despair and suicide, Alicia. Men are an unhappy lot. They are bored with themselves and the world and end up hating us once they've used us up. They are like children in need of the female breast. They are lonely for their mothers. I feel sorry for them, Alicia, but I don't need any man. And Pale Moon doesn't need to get pregnant by some man. Men rob women of their dreams. And the children are chains they shackle us with."

Many of the Indian women agreed with Yellow Rose, and surprising as it might have been to Alicia, many of the women wished they didn't have to put up with men who claimed to be macho while they cried like babies for the female teat that allowed them to forget they were of this planet.

Evening was falling. Fires were burning. Women were cooking. Men were drinking. Children were beating up on each other. A lonely guitarist was playing a sad song. Alicia ate her frijoles and tortillas, her body aching from the work she had done that day. She suddenly realized that no one should have to work in these orchards or fields, picking fruits and vegetables like giant locusts. There ought to be machines to do this sort of menial work, while the men and women could and should enjoy their free time to improve their minds and souls with study.

Kyle's figure appeared in the darkness across her way. He spoke to one of the Mexican girls and drove off with her. Alicia wondered how many of these girls had tasted hamburgers and fries. No sooner had she raised mankind from its primitive state than she threw the men and women back into their caves and allowed them to be devoured by dinosaurs. Even with all the time on their hands, especially men like Kyle and the obese man, they would do nothing and learn nothing. And why should they learn anything when they had money?

Alicia thought she might want to go to college like Pale Moon. As she entertained this thought, a tall young man with a sheep on his shoulders appeared before her. He stood in his own silence and said nothing to her. Yellow Rose and Pale Moon, seeing the young man, ran towards him and embraced him and the sheep.

"You have stolen the sheep?" Yellow Rose asked.

The young man, who was Running Antelope, didn't answer his mother. Alicia had expected him to answer her.

"It doesn't matter, Mama," Pale Moon said as she took the animal to the other women.

"I won't eat any of the white man's stolen sheep," Yellow Rose insisted.

Pale Moon and the other Indian women preyed on the sheep and then cut the animal into pieces that they cooked on the fire to rid themselves of the evidence.

Running Antelope ate some frijoles and tortillas near Alicia by the fire, chewing in silence. Alicia had expected to hear a gentle word caress his lips, but this man, unlike the men she had known, didn't even look up at her. His eyes were swimming in the hot embers of the fire, as if they were studying them. She decided he was preoccupied with some important thought.

"You shouldn't have stolen the sheep," Alicia said out of the blue.

Running Antelope looked up at her. His eyes in the reflection of the fire appeared like two wounded doves unable to take flight.

S. Leconte

"Food makes people act like animals. They will kill for food. If they have food, they will behave like human beings," he said as if he were reading one of his history books.

"They will kill even if they have food," Alicia said, remembering the obese man and others of his kind.

"Jesus! I bring a sheep to you all, and you give me the third degree. What the hell did I do!?"

"You stole, my son. And Alicia is right."

"I don't need her to tell me what I get for you. Nobody appreciates what I try to do! And do you know why all your men drink? Do you? Because of you women. You have taken away their power. You tell them not to steal or kill!"

"Enough!" Yellow Rose cried out.

"If you want to do something, organize these people and put these owners out of business," she continued.

"I have tried that. I have, and you saw how they laughed at me."

"And their laughter defeated you? My son, my poor son, I remember when you were a boy, you would come from school crying because others had picked on you. And what did I used to tell you?"

"To go out and fight another day."

"These white men must be taught over and over again, my son, that we are not their slaves. We came into this world as they did, from a woman's womb. We were born to enjoy the same fruit of the same tree."

"Mama, you should have been a philosopher."

"You've read too many books, Running Antelope," Pale Moon said, laughing.

The women washed the dishes and stored the cooked lamb. Alicia and Pale Moon took some of the cooked meat even though Yellow Rose wouldn't touch any of it. Alicia had decided that a stolen but dead sheep couldn't be returned to its owner and that meat shouldn't be wasted, not even out of principle. She would partake of the meat and feed her body on the sins of Running Antelope.

The men and women lay down to sleep. The fires were dying. The air continued to stifle. The lonely guitar had been wrapped in a rag and stored away. Alicia couldn't sleep, perhaps because the moon was full. Running Antelope was sitting by the dying fire before his mother's tent, absorbed in thought. Alicia got up and sat with this man, who could have been a mere statue if she hadn't known that he was made of flesh and blood. Without speaking, Running Antelope's body spoke of great frustration that came from the pain of wanting to be like his ancestors. There was something noble in his face. She had seen his long face, high cheekbones, serious eyes, aquiline nose and angry mouth in a magazine ad, in which a man, wearing musk, was staring at the moon while a woman knelt at his feet, her arms wrapped around his legs. Alicia didn't want to be that woman kneeling at a man's feet; nor did she want a man, like Kyle, to kneel at her feet, repeating empty words and phrases as if he were before God Himself.

Alicia knew intuitively that Running Antelope wanted to improve the lot of the people, but the people seemed satisfied with the new salami sandwiches. Running Antelope had spoken to many of the men and women in the many fields and orchards along the river, only to be met with opposition from those who continued to go hungry. They didn't want to lose their jobs! They didn't want to lose the little food and money they were getting. Life was that simple when you lived like a locust eating leaves on the sly.

To Running Antelope, men and women were like ants that obeyed the queen of the anthill. She owned each grain of dirt and the worker ants were sent out to forage for food to feed the belly of the queen who grew fatter and fatter, while the masses ate what was left over although they had done the tunneling, the foraging, and killing of those outside the group.

"The only way you'll get them on your side is if you throw them a pachanga (party). Their hearts cannot be moved when they are already sad. You must raise their spirits and then talk to them."

"You women think you're so wise," he said and ran off into the dark.

"I was trying to help!" she cried out.

Some voices shushed her down, and she sat a while against the trunk of a tree. Alicia had seen men come through her village. They all had come with the same revolutionary message, trying to incite the men to rob, kill and overthrow the government. Until the day she died her grandmother used to say that nothing had changed and that nothing would change. But words were empty when not accompanied with deeds. Running Antelope would have to prove himself before he could be trusted.

Alicia had no dream that night. She didn't dream of Running Antelope kissing her. She didn't make love or think of making love, which she knew existed in real life and especially in the movies and television. She wanted to be respected for her thoughts, and so far Running Antelope had insulted her by negating her as a woman. She was glad he had said nothing kind earlier or she might have begun to like him. How could she like a man who seemed to hate women in his heart? How could he prove his love to his mother? The stolen sheep was one such act denied him by Yellow Rose, who would eat of the stolen lamb, but not in front of her son. As Alicia ate of the lamb for the next few days, she prayed, but not to God, that Running Antelope would return with more lamb. Even Yellow Rose missed her son and said, "The lamb is good even if it is stolen. My son is good, but he shouldn't steal."

"Mama, the lamb ate grass from our stolen land. The lamb must be ours," Pale Moon said, and all the women agreed and laughed.

"You are right, Pale Moon. We must tell Running Antelope to get us more of this lamb."

"I never thought of it that way," Alicia said. She couldn't wait for Running Antelope to return so that she could tell him of the idea the women had come up with to save his honor.

-9-

What Does Karl Marx Know Anyway?

Yellow Rose had delivered several babies among the young Mexican girls almost within one week. The girls were all unmarried, and like Santa María, claimed they were virgins who had not had sex with anyone. Not everyone knew better. Many still believed in good old-fashioned miracles in spite of all the scientific data that for the most part remained out of their reach. They believed in dreams and that dreams were a reflection of this reality. The fathers of these daughters demanded to know if they had perhaps sinned in their dreams. The girls insisted that their dreams had been totally pure and filled with salami sandwiches and oranges. The mothers of these daughters were not so gullible, but didn't question the dreams, reality, or anything else, preferring to save the honor of their daughters. Saints are not beyond sinning. They often rape young women in their sleep. After all, how could the Heavens have become so populated?

Yellow Rose knelt near the Mexican girl while Alicia sat by her side translating. Juana's father stood above them, screaming to know how such a dishonorable thing could have happened. Her mother yelled at him to be quiet or he would cause the baby to be born deaf if he came into this world listening to his shouting. Juana's face and body were drowning in sweat, her face wrinkled in pain, her mouth twisted and bloody. Juana's father didn't believe in miracles or dreams. He had been an avid reader of Reader's Digest in translation and was up on the latest scientific information: men and their penises got women pregnant. He shouted the information. Juana broke down and shouted in despair that she had gotten pregnant because of the hamburger she had eaten. Alicia understood.

"Nobody can get pregnant eating hamburger meat!" Juana's thin father insisted.

"Old man, find it in those books where it says hamburger doesn't!" Juana's plump mother demanded.

"How could she have eaten hamburger meat, when all we eat is salami sandwiches and frijoles?"

"Maybe she ate some in her dream."

Juana cried out that she had seen a large hamburger palace and a young man had beckoned her to enter the palace where he fed her all the hamburger she could eat and a chocolate milkshake to top it all off.

"Maybe I could dream of such a place and we would never have to wake up! What do you take me for, a fool? Miguel dreamt of owning a truck. You don't see him driving one, do you?" Juana's father would bury the issue.

"You know Miguel, old man. He drives like a drunk burro, and he probably wrecked the truck at the intersection before he could drive out of the dream. God provides in our dreams. Usually I ask for chicken, and He gives it to me. Of course, He is sometimes stingy and gives me only wings. Please, dear God, send me a thigh or breast my way," Juana's mother said, looking up as she crossed herself.

While Juana's mother and father were having another of their philosophical arguments, Yellow Rose was holding a child's head in her hands, its hair black and bloody, but beautiful as any animal breaking into the light of life. Juana was pushing with all her might, cursing the hamburger, while Alicia held her hand and wiped her forehead. The baby's body flowed out of Juana's womb like a fish at the end of its swim, crossing the shore to become a human being. Alicia smiled and almost cried when she heard the child's first helpless cry. Yellow Rose bathed the child clean, while Juana's mother, who had kicked the old man out to figure out the laws of pregnancy, was cleaning up her own daughter. Juana's face expressed nothing but relief, not the love that should have been written in her eyes and mouth for the innocent life that she now wanted dead.

Juana had told Alicia one day that she had wanted to have an abortion, but the night she had thought what she considered an evil thought, a giant dragon popped into her dream along with a young man named Miguel. He was carrying a sword and shouting at the dragon. Apparently the dragon had come to take another child as sacrifice, and Juana had stood in her dream handing her child over into the dragon's fiery mouth. Then Miguel, whom Juana had loved in her dreams, popped out of the corner of the cave and slashed the dragon to pieces. Miguel was covered with greenish blood. He stood before her, armor and sword dripping green and saying, "Juana, it is wrong to kill children."

Juana wanted to give the child up, preferably to rich people who could give it a better future. At the moment, all the boy named Miguelito could look forward to was picking oranges, spinach, and lettuce and becoming one of the locust people for the rest of his life.

Alicia could offer no solution to Juana's situation. The only thing she could hope for would be to marry a rich man or one who had his head in the clouds. But Alicia didn't mention any rich husband to Juana. Instead she told her to love the child and bring him up to be a decent human being. Juana looked up at Alicia as if she were an alien fallen from a strange planet. How could she love this child born out of a hamburger and chocolate milkshake? Juana cursed herself for having succumbed to temptation, which no amount of prayer, forgiveness, or confession could erase because the devil himself would come every morning and deliver the salami sandwiches with the obese man.

Alicia, Juana told her, was a fool for believing in decency. She would bring up her child to steal and kill the gringos, if need be, to make a better life for itself. Hearing such violent talk from an otherwise peaceful girl frightened Alicia. How could she bring up a child to believe in theft and murder? It was easy because the child would learn from the other children who stole not oranges, other fruits, and vegetables but spare tires and those not so spare from various parts of the camp until none of the peons had any tires on their cars or trucks. Now they were truly stuck until they collected enough money to buy new tires to take them to new fields. But their sons were not as malicious as they seemed, especially not to their own kind. To get the cars and trucks back on the road to cotton and spinach fields, these loyal sons "found" new tires in town to match even the oldest models their fathers had driven since God kicked Adam and Eve out of His precious garden. If this wasn't love, what was? Unfortunately, love can and does get people in trouble. Some, but not all of the sons, were arrested for "auto theft."

The parents of these loyal sons were incensed by these accusations. How could their "hijitos" have stolen cars when all they could hardly carry off were tires? And who said they had stolen these tires? Who had seen their little "hijitos" steal? Where were the witnesses? And just because they had been caught red-handed with tires, didn't mean they had stolen them. Gringos have no imagination! Everything has to be a matter of fact, spelled by laws. How can they believe in God? Is He a mechanic in a garage? No, God is above us all. He is the man who makes magic. He is the man who can get women pregnant when the men are tired from working in the fields. He is the man with a giant wrench who loosens screws and nuts and bolts and floods the streets with loose tires. Have the gringos not heard of the expression "Ask and you shall get what you want?" So they asked for tires and it rained tires.

Lucky for their sons, the business community intervened and promised to create jobs for the youths. Many were hired in garages, of all places. The people in town thought all the tires would disappear from the face of the earth. Tires in this part of the world were almost as sacred as beer and smokes, not to mention God, flag, and country. Wheels were what kept cars and trucks running, especially trucks. Wheels were the source of their livelihood. Wheels were like the horses men used to ride. And even these men agreed that a lame car was of no use to the rider. They demanded that some of the "hijitos" be hanged properly. Lynching was such a primitive thing to do. Proper hanging should have been decreed by the judge. Lucky for the sons, the judge had some Hispanic blood that flowed through his veins and he too believed that trees often ran into cars and caused accidents. He believed in the magic that made this world.

Some of the sons were not so fortunate and were shot like roadrunners by the owners who caught their wheels in flight.

Pepito, a six-year old, had been murdered by one such hunter and was buried in a field by the side of road like a small seed, wrapped in his favorite calico blanket. Alicia had stood with the others. The mother was moaning and beating her breast, while the women wrapped around her like flowers to comfort with their aromas. The men said nothing, except after

the funeral. Many told their sons to leave tires alone. Tires
were sacred to the gringos like horses used to be. This would-
n't have happened if they hadn't stolen tires in the first place!
The young boys called the men "old farts!" and "pendejos!"
who lived in another century. They were not about to end up
like their fathers, peons to the gringos. They would rather die
fighting for what they believed.

Juana claimed she had Zapata and Villa blood flowing
through her veins and that Miguelito would slay dragons not
only in her dreams. Juana too believed her son would fight for
what he believed in. Alicia asked her what he would believe in.
Juana couldn't believe her ears. How could Alicia not know
what her son would believe in? She yelled at Alicia and told
her to work another ten years picking fruits and vegetables, eat
a hamburger and get pregnant. Then she would know what to
believe in. Freedom! ¡Libertad!

Running Antelope had come back from Yale full of libertad he had read about in books, especially the kind of books
he should have left alone. When he told her that in Das
Kapital, Karl Marx promoted a thing called communism, she
knew immediately that he was on the wrong track. When she
made the mistake of asking him what the book really said,
Running Antelope spent hours speaking and explaining the
economic theories that Karl had written down to change
mankind. Alicia thought she had heard this message in church
but said nothing for fear he would tell her that she understood
nothing because she was a woman.

Although Alicia spent hours listening to Running
Antelope and understood what he was trying to do, she didn't
fall in love with him because he was trying to appear intelligent. Alicia thought he had read far too many books and had
forgotten how to talk to normal people as he tried to apply

theory to people instead of listening to the people and their needs. Running Antelope, a born but lost leader, assumed what was best for the people of the orchards.

"The land belonged to us and should be given back to us," he yelled.

Alicia, who had heard Manhattan was once Indian land, asked what it should become with its large skyscrapers. Running Antelope wanted to send all immigrants back to their countries and raze the buildings down to the ground. God might have agreed with him and razed these towers of Babel to rubble, but Running Antelope wasn't all anti-technology. He thought television would one day replace man's head, and that children would be born with TV antennas instead of ears. They would have no minds and they would forget how to read. They would forget how to grow food or build houses, and they would need someone to lead them out of nothingness. Alicia had seen this phenomenon in her own village, and all of a sudden she thought that Running Antelope was someone with a vision. The armor he had built around himself melted, and she saw a helpless little boy trying to save himself in a world that was swallowing him up.

Alicia mentioned the fact that television had put her village to sleep and that children now thought that milk came from a bottle because there were no cows to remind them of the origin of milk. Running Antelope didn't respond to her statement.

"And the telephone and computers will take away what's left of our language. Do you know that many of our children don't speak the language of our ancestors," he said.

Alicia rose to her feet and walked away, leaving Running Antelope to his own speech until he realized that he was alone. She knew he would follow her if she ignored him. Men do not like to be ignored by women, especially when they are doing the talking. Having listened to him, Alicia decided that all men thought they should be taken seriously no matter what trite matter they were spouting off. Even when they said they loved women, their love was more important. If a woman dared say she loved a man, he always said he was hungry or that he needed to take a piss.

Alicia had seen her mother humiliate herself before a man whom she had loved beyond the definition of love. Her mother would wash, iron, and put the clothes on the man as if he were a small doll. She would cut his vegetables, meat, fruit, and feed him all this exotic food because he hated frijoles and tortillas. Not all Mexicans are fond of them. Later her mother disclosed that the man was of German origin because his penis could only function when the cuckoo clock struck nine. There was nothing her mother wouldn't do to please him. Anytime she said something, he would dismiss her by contradicting her statements, but when he said, "¡Yo te quiero!" (I love you!), his "yo" stood straight like a soldier in uniform demanding immediate attention. Alicia wondered if men thought they were more important than women because they were in possession of a penis.

Running Antelope wondered if he had said something wrong. Alicia had heard this immediate reaction from José, Kyle and other men, who do not listen to women or other men for that matter unless these men are saying something they want to hear. Alicia turned around and said something she didn't regret.

"Why do you think you can change the world? Maybe I should ask why you should change the world?"

"This world should change because there are so many things wrong with it," he answered.

"I asked you why you should change it? Why you?"

"Because I hate what I see. Karl . . . "

"I don't want to hear any more theories about that man. From the words you have used, this Karl must not have loved anyone."

"He loved humanity."

"He must have hated his family. His poor wife must have had to be quiet because she couldn't disturb him. I can see him sitting at his desk writing his book while his children have to tiptoe so that the man's thoughts are not broken. Of course, the woman would cook his meals. A thinking man must be fed or his brains will shrivel! And after a good meal, she must light his cigar and then she probably has to sit and listen to all the pages he has scribbled. And she, of course, has to agree with his every word to make his ego feel good. Is that all a woman is, a reflection of or receptacle for man's thoughts!? Is that what you want out of a woman?"

"What's got into you?"

"I am mad! Mad because all you men can say is, 'What's got into you?' You don't bother to ask why I am speaking the way I am."

"I am sorry!" he said as he touched her shoulder with his hand, but quickly removed it as if she were either a piece of ice or a stove too hot to handle. Alicia wondered if he had withdrawn his apology along with his hand.

"Are you afraid of women?"

"No!"

"Why did you answer that way?"

"Because I don't want you to dig into my soul or pry."

"I don't want to pry! I won't speak anymore then!"

Alicia knew that silence usually made men think, and Running Antelope, like all men, couldn't stand the silence coming from a woman. He had to break it with words. He had to smash the water as if it were glass to create ripples, to be heard, to remind himself and others that he was alive. But Running Antelope could play the game as well. He remained silent with her and then instead of rambling the continuing episodes of Karl's Utopia or Heaven on Earth, which Alicia knew would never work, he touched her hand, and tears, real tears, that no man had yet shed for her, came flowing from his eyes.

Alicia touched his cheeks and wiped the tears with her fingers, squeezing each tear as if it were a precious pearl come from an invisible but enchanting ocean, which she had yet to see. Each tear spoke of the pain Running Antelope was feeling. The stream seemed endless. Then he opened his mouth and he spoke gently without the oratorical style of politicians who had come through her village. He mentioned that he had once been in love with a young woman from his tribe. He had loved her as he had never loved anyone. He had given of his heart and soul. He had left no thought unturned, no feeling unsaid, until she could read him like a book, but she remained quiet and seemed to calculate his death. One day she left the reservation with a travelling salesman who could give her all the pots and pans she would need in her life. A month later she came back to the reservation and begged him to marry her. But by then the coals in his heart had cooled, and the passion had died until he went to college and read Karl.

Alicia discovered that underneath Karl lay a dead woman, and that Das Kapital had become her tombstone. To reach that passion and to put new coals into the chambers of his heart, she would have to resuscitate the dead woman and crawl into her shell and perhaps take on her name. Maybe not!

As she listened to his woeful tale, she now felt she understood him a little more, but there she was listening again and feeling grateful for having done so. Alicia felt like a mother. Men always marry their mothers. Some even beat them. Others kill them. Running Antelope loved his mother as he would love the woman he married. Then he asked her, "What is a pachanga, Alicia? Tell me how I can turn the tide of history around?"

That night as she lay alone, she felt a pride she had never experienced in her life.

-10-

What is a Pachanga?

Alicia explained to Running Antelope that pachangas (lively parties) in her country across the river had changed the course of history. It was during such pachangas that angels smiled upon the people and brought them gifts wanted and unwanted. It was a time for women to get pregnant and men to propose marriage because they were drunk on tequila. It was a time of vengeance. Pepe's father went out into the night drunk out of his mind and murdered Mr. Sanchez's pig because he had complimented his wife on her looks. It was during one of these pachangas that the Mexican revolution (one of many) started out of control. There would be a lot of eating, laughter and music, and dancing. It would be fun.

Alicia reassured Running Antelope that gifts in the name of love were always answered in kind. People had good hearts and always remembered the good done them. Running Antelope wanted to help these people to raise themselves out of the poverty that was stifling growth. Pretty soon they would start thinking they were salami sandwiches themselves. How could he then convince a salami sandwich that it was a human being? People would remember him for throwing this pachanga, and he would then be able to lead them into battle against the obese man, the thin woman, and their son.

Running Antelope couldn't help but be enthusiastic. He was ready to lead the people out of the orchards onto the highway that led back to the Garden of Eden if need be. Alicia was happy to see him so excited and couldn't wait to eat something other than frijoles. Even though she had objected to his stealing the obese man's sheep earlier on, she had tasted the lamb of God and liked it, especially with garlic and salsa picante that permeated the air and nostrils of onlookers waiting with tongues hanging out like dogs', hungry to devour the lamb of God but leave His bones intact to resurrect Himself when miracles are needed. She suggested that Running Antelope "find" a few "stray sheep" and roast them on a spit.

Running Antelope, hearing Alicia make such a bold statement, was taken aback and surprised. A look of fear quickly invaded his eyes and mouth as he stood numbed by her words, which could land him in jail. He may have been an activist and a union organizer, but he was no martyr. He was not ready to be lynched or spend twenty years in jail (two years per sheep). You see, Alicia had ordered ten large sheep that would go noticed even by the blind Basque shepherd, who had already complained about missing sheep to the obese man, who dismissed his complaints by saying, "Coyotes have to eat too!" The blind Basque shepherd hadn't minded the first few sheep, but when the "bahs" began to diminish in intensity and frequency, he decided to buy a shotgun with his hard-earned money and protect his assets. After all, if he had no sheep to guard, he would be out of a job, and what other job could a blind shepherd find in this day and age? The idea of selling pencils on some street corner probably didn't appeal to him.

When Running Antelope mentioned the blind Basque shepherd and his newly purchased shotgun, Alicia was beginning to lose respect for the man who was appearing less brave and heroic by the second. He feared for his life, unlike the snake or fox, and to Alicia fear for one's life was something worse than cowardice. If this man were ever to declare his love for her, she would have to remind him of his manhood. How can the course of history be changed without people taking a risk?

Running Antelope left her side, feeling guilty and ready to lead the people perhaps because he wanted to have his name entered in the annals of history books, which he no longer read because they were full of lies. Perhaps he wanted to lead the people to impress Alicia? Men will do silly things to unlock women's hearts and become their servants, slaves, tormentors, torturers, etc., in the name of love. All Alicia wanted was ten sheep for the pachanga. As Running Antelope was about to vanish into the dark of night, she yelled, "Don't forget the tequila, frijoles for the chile, and the hot peppers!" Alicia knew in her heart that Running Antelope would not fail her.

Alicia didn't want to jeopardize Running Antelope's endeavors, although she wanted to tell everyone that he was going to throw a pachanga. Unable to keep her tongue in check, Alicia let it slip out to Pale Moon that her brother was out rounding up sheep for a fiesta to show the people what freedoms they were missing. Pale Moon, who was a wagger girl herself, told her mother that Running Antelope had gone to steal more sheep for a fiesta suggested by Alicia. When Yellow Rose heard this, she flew into a rage for a good reason.

"Are you trying to get my son killed!?"

Alicia was surprised to hear such an accusation come from the woman who had cared for her.

"No!" she answered.

"My son is crazy with love for you. Do you know that?"

"No!"

"Well, he is! And you send your future husband out for sheep! To steal sheep!"

"I'm sorry I sent him out to steal, but a pachanga could change the course of history."

"What history? What are you talking about, Alicia? Nothing changes in history. Everything is the same here. We are born, we eat, we give birth to our own kind and die."

"But you can't eat frijoles all your life! And you ate the lamb and liked it!"

"Yes, I did like it. But it is wrong to eat such lamb when it isn't ours!"

"But the obese man steals from our bodies."

"I'm not talking about stealing. Stealing is easy. You can live with that. Men can live with stealing. It's eating the lamb they won't be able to live with. You see, Alicia, when I ate that one piece of lamb, it tasted so very good that my soul wanted more. That night my body ached, and my soul soared to the heavens where there were large open plains and many many sheep. And I was happy to be in this heaven. Then I became hungry in my dream. I thought to myself, 'Why should I eat frijoles, when I can have the lamb of God!?' So I ran after the sheep, but I couldn't even come close to one. Then a man with two large wings and a shotgun in hand stood before me and asked me who had let me through the gates of Heaven. I told him that I didn't know. He pointed the shotgun at me and just as he pulled the trigger I fell through a dark hole and landed back in my tent. The sheep will only tease our mouths and souls. They aren't for us."

"But the people need a taste of the lamb to dream, Yellow Rose. And what's wrong with a pachanga?"

"It's wrong to cause despair. Men are not fish. You can't play with them by dangling bait to make them dream, Alicia. They have to want to change themselves."

"But how will Running Antelope lead these people to victory?"

"You are beginning to talk nonsense as he does! There is no such thing as victory, Alicia!"

"But my mother said that leaders were born out of pachangas."

"Pachangas don't make leaders. They were leaders before the music started. If you love my son . . . "

"I never said I did. And whatever he has been saying about me is wrong. I never promised to become his wife." Alicia cried out, angry and frustrated because Running Antelope was either a liar or living in a dream world, because he hadn't mentioned his love to her, because he was a mama's boy, because he wasn't a born leader, because he was a pachanga hater like his mother, because he was a coward, because he didn't trust her, because he had entered her heart and ruined her dream of finding herself a millionaire husband and changing the course of history in her village.

After speaking to Yellow Rose, Alicia no longer felt in the mood for a pachanga. She had dreamt of dancing with Running Antelope, who would have to be taught how to dance whether he liked it or not. She didn't, however, hope that the blind Basque would shoot him. Alicia was not the type of woman who could wish death to the one she loved. She wasn't, however, eager to forget the feeling she had experienced as she tried to deny her love for Running Antelope, which had yet to be defined. Should he succeed in stealing the ten sheep and in providing the tequila for the workers, it would be a start in the right direction. Words alone couldn't define love. Dictionaries failed where life began. And if Running Antelope should be wounded, Alicia would love him even more in spite of denying it. Of course, she didn't want anything to happen to him and would hate herself for having thought of him wounded by the blind Basque.

Alicia felt like running into the dark to tell Running Antelope to forget all about the pachanga, but Pale Moon had the jump on her and had wagged all over camp that her brave big brother was going to throw a fiesta for everyone in the orchard. And once a pachanga is in the works, there is no going back.

The next day she went to work as did all the others, who couldn't wait to taste the sweet garlicky lamb of God roasted on a spit over mesquite. Their mouths could already taste the meat, and this prevented them from working as hard as they usually did. The oranges seemed to dangle out of their reach like elusive suns. Their baskets seemed to remain empty for hours, their hands almost numb to the reality before them. The obese man and his son watched the slow motion picking and yelled at the peons because the orange juice couldn't wait to be squeezed into people's glasses. The obese man threatened to take their salami sandwiches away if they didn't speed up their picking. No one heard him. They were already sitting down to the lamb feast and tequila and telling stories that had already been told. When the afternoon sun rolled over, the men didn't return to work. Instead, they waited in the shade of oak shrubs and stared at the highway like hopeless pilgrims waiting for a sign from above. They were birds without wings. Yet, there was a twinkling of hope in the deep recesses of their eyes. They knew something would happen.

Alicia picked oranges in a daze, unable to grasp the fruit from the tree. She wondered if Running Antelope would come back at all and if he did, would he bring the ten sheep and tequila. She, too, stared at the road, waiting to see dust rise with the news of a rider come to save the day. Everyone seemed dead, except for Yellow Rose, who had put the lamb in her head out to pasture. Perhaps she was right, Alicia thought; hope and dreams can bring men and women so low that the next dream might bring despair and lead to suicide.

Yellow Rose, however, also looked at the road as she picked oranges like a woman on fire. Alicia knew that she was wait-

ing for her son to return, not with the sheep and tequila. Alicia
felt suddenly guilty and wished she had never mentioned the
word sheep. She shouldn't have suggested that Running
Antelope steal anything. The taste of lamb turned sour in her
mouth as she saw him lying near the sheep. His body was rid-
dled with bullets, bleeding like a sieve. The man she might be
in love with was dead! Alicia's face was covered with sweat and
tears as she threw herself on his body to protect him from the
vultures that were eager to carry his organs and other body
parts to the four corners of Texas.

It was evening, but no one was yelling; no one was fixing
frijoles; no one was cursing. They were waiting in the light of
bonfires for a miracle to happen. She wanted to go and reas-
sure them that Running Antelope was a man of his word and
that there would be a pachanga. But she knew if she did, they
would curse her for putting the idea of a pachanga into their
heads. But what is a man without dreams, she thought, even
if the dream might never come true? Dreaming of the lamb of
God and tasting its meat in a dream pachanga was as good as
tasting the real lamb, and if they didn't dream, they would
never taste the lamb. And that would be a loss!

Yellow Rose was the only person moving. She stirred the
pot of frijoles in silence, staring at Alicia. She understood the
implication of her stare. When the frijoles were cooked, Yellow
Rose handed Alicia and Pale Moon each a bowlful, but neither
of them could eat.

Then lights, two small lights, appeared on the highway.
One head rose out of hopelessness and gave rise to the others,
who also noticed the lights. There was guarded expectation in
their still slow motion. It was useless to spend energy on hope
that would never be realized. Someone with good night vision
called the vehicle a truck. Someone with good hearing
thought she had gone deaf because she couldn't hear the
baahing of sheep. Someone with the best, keenest sense of

smell in Texas, a gringo who claimed to be Mexican because his name happened to be Villa, said aloud that the truck wasn't carrying any tequila. But the people hushed this false prophet quickly. They wanted to see everything for themselves. The truck could have veered to the left where there was a road that led away from the orchard or right to the obese man's house, but it didn't. Instead, the lights went out and the motor seemed to have died. There was nothing like hope hanged over and over again with multiple reprieves!

Just as the men were about to return to their ghostly selves near the fires, Running Antelope emerged out of the darkness with a skinned lamb on his shoulders. Alicia suddenly knew she was in love with the man standing proudly next to the men who were patting the lamb on the back. Several of the men went and got the other sheep and several cases of tequila, and someone drove the truck away.

Yellow Rose smiled at her son's return. Alicia's heart was gladdened because her hand had touched her face, and the touch meant more than words of forgiveness. The touch brought her closer to the woman who might become her mother-in-law, although Alicia wasn't sure this feeling of love was right for her. She was flesh and blood and capable of making up her own mind.

The men wrapped the lambs of God on the spits and began drinking tequila while the women stirred salsa, frijoles, and any food that they might have been hoarding. The lamb wouldn't be ready until the next day, but this was a pachanga, and they would wait forever if need be for the lamb to be cooked. The men were happy to let the tequila thin their blood. The lamb could wait. They had dreams of their own.

While a lonely guitar played happy tunes and couples danced, stomping their feet into the clay as if to squash cockroaches, Running Antelope, who had concluded his business, walked over to his mother. She hugged her son as if he had just returned from the house of the dead. Then he walked over to Alicia and attempted to touch her shoulder. She flinched like a wild mare unused to the human touch, and he withdrew his hand as if he had touched something too hot to handle. Alicia was staring at the lamb with her back to Running Antelope. She didn't know why she was being so cold to him. She had at first wanted to hug him for having returned safely, but instead, she was angry because he could have been killed, not remembering that it was she who had suggested the pachanga in the first place, not to mention the nearly dozen sheep she told him to steal. Running Antelope moved away from her and joined the men at the various fires. He had organized the pachanga to feed their bellies with lamb, their blood with tequila, and their minds with ideas.

After cooling off, Alicia joined Running Antelope to act as interpreter and to explain to the men and women what he was trying to do. He told them that the people who worked the land, not the owner, owned the land. The oranges they picked belonged to the person who picked them. The sheep belonged to the man brave enough to take them. The bull belonged to the bullfighter once he killed it. These words didn't go over their heads. They now understood what he was saying until he brought up the word "union." He told them that unions organized strikes and made demands for higher pay. Many agreed to join the union and to fight the tyranny of the obese man. They were already tired of his salami sandwiches, just as they had gotten tired of the bologna sandwiches. Why shouldn't they eat lamb every day?

As Running Antelope had quelled their hunger, he had raised their spirits with dreams of a better life that the drunken voices applauded.

"I could never get tired of lamb."

"Me neither."

"You get tired of your wife, José! Why shouldn't you get tired of lamb?"

"You're drunk, Pepe. And when you drink, you always lie!"

"I don't lie! Listen to me!"

"Eat and shut up, Pepe. Can't you have a good time? You always tell us it's going to rain, but it never does. You pray for rain because you don't like the sun, not that we like it either. We could use some rain."

"José, if we go on strike, the fat man will hire those waiting at the gates. And José, they will eat dirt instead of bologna sandwiches."

"Pepe, eat some lamb!"

"I don't want any. And if we demand higher wages, then wouldn't we have to pay higher prices for our own oranges?"

"Pepe, what kind of foolishness are you talking about? Do we ever buy oranges?"

Everyone laughed at Pepe, who walked away from the party that lasted all weekend. The men had promised Running Antelope they would start organizing their first strike. "¡Huelga! ¡Huelga! ¡Huelga! (Strike!)" they shouted as they practiced their striking chant. Running Antelope, hearing the voice of the people fill his heart, was ecstatic, and Alicia could feel a rush of adrenaline along her spine. She, too, felt alive. That night Running Antelope kissed her, but didn't attempt to make love to her. Alicia was both disappointed and relieved that she was still a virgin in the morning.

-11-
What Does a Strawberry Taste Like?

Alicia sat up with Running Antelope all night. He was so excited about the day to come that he forgot to tell her about the stars up above and a thing called love. She listened, as his mother had listened to him when he was a boy. Although she wanted to see him succeed in organizing the strike, she wished that he would pay attention to her. She felt troubled as she realized that now that a man like Running Antelope was cold to her, she wanted him to say the silly things other men would have said. She wanted to hear anything that had to do with love, not the upcoming strike.

Running Antelope was like most men, Alicia thought, self-centered babies who needed to stand in the limelight. He wanted to hear, "¡Huelga! ¡Huelga! ¡Huelga!" echo through the orchards and lead the men to victory against the obese man and his son. There was anger in his voice as he spoke of taking their land and forming a community of farmers who would own the land and share the profits as Karl had written. Alicia was tired of hearing about Karl and his economic theory, but she kept her mouth shut. There was vengeance in his heart as he spoke of burning down the obese man's house to erase the tyranny the thin woman had enjoyed for years. He would hang the obese men who lived along the river and who exploited the poor as they had been exploited all through the centuries, since the beginning of time. Running Antelope would change all of that.

Alicia imagined a revolution unfolding before her eyes as he painted the countryside with blood. She was frightened by this kind of talk and told him that he had no right to kill anyone.

"Why are you so upset, Alicia?"

"Because of the way you are talking! You cannot set yourself as judge and kill whoever you want!"

"It's not what I want. And besides, I was just speaking in metaphors."

"What's a metaphor? Why do you use words that could get you killed?"

"A metaphor is . . . "

"I don't want to hear it. I have listened to you all night. I like to listen to you, don't get me wrong, but my ears are aching from all your talking. Forget Karl and the strike, Running Antelope, just for ten minutes, and say something I will understand."

"What do you want to understand?"

"You must be kidding!"

"Alicia, you're speaking in circles!"

"I'm trying to get you to . . . "

"You want to hear words about love, is that it?"

"No, not really, but since you mentioned it, it wouldn't be a bad idea if you said something nice."

"You women always want to hear about love. Alicia, these are turbulent times, and love must be put on hold. Do you want me to feed you lies like the white man? Do you want me to create dreams for you? I am out of dreams. I have no dream house for you! No kids or dogs or lawns! Besides, I must dedicate myself to these men and women. This morning will be a turning point in their lives, Alicia! Feel the air! It's trembling! It's ready to blow away the fat man and his son!"

Alicia fell asleep in Running Antelope's arms, cradled against his chest, and the warmth coming from his body melted the anger she had felt earlier. With her heart to his she heard the galloping of wild horses rumble through her own body. His heart was strong, capable of love, but Alicia knew she would have to draw blood from the well to get him to express his feelings. And it wasn't only women who needed to hear they were loved! Running Antelope, she thought, needed it most. It was for that reason he wanted to lead men into battle. To have their approval and love.

When morning came, Alicia found herself on the sandy ground, Running Antelope absent from her side. She noticed the men and women stirring, trucks and station wagons being loaded. Where was everyone going? Running Antelope was screaming at the men, whose heads were aching from last night's tequila. But dreams and imagination are always best when fueled and fermented by tequila or any other one hundred-proof-drink. They had had their strike last night as they chanted, "¡Huelga! ¡Huelga! ¡Huelga!" over food and drink.

"It was a great strike, Running Antelope!" one still unsober mind exclaimed, his hands striking an imaginary obese man in the face.

"We should do it again!"

"You sure know how to throw a pachanga!"

"And did you see the fat man cry before we hanged him!?"

"And how his guts fell out when we opened him up!"

"But there was no gold in his stomach like you said there would be!"

"I knew that. Everybody knows there's no gold, just shit!"

"So why did you cut off his balls!?"

"They say they're worth their weight in gold."

"Balls are balls!"

"You don't know much about balls. My father ate pig's balls, bull's balls, and he was the most manly man in the village. And when they wanted a man, they could come to him because he had balls! And if I eat the fat man's balls, I might get rich like he was!"

"But you gave me your word!" Running Antelope cried out. "I almost got shot by the blind Basque for stealing sheep so that you could eat of the lamb!" he continued.

"The lamb was great, hombre! And we all admire you. You are the bravest man we have known in a long time."

"The bravest! Hurrah! Hurrah!" everyone yelled.

"You don't understand. We must strike against the fat man and make our demands."

"The old days are over, hombre. Villa and Zapata cannot be resurrected."

"¡Viva Villa!" the men cried out.

"We live in the twentieth century. Soon we will be in the twenty-first. We have learned that some of us are meant to eat dirt. So here we are!"

"But we can change things. You can have a better life for your wives and children. Don't you want to eat strawberries once in a while?"

"We will eat them tomorrow."

Alicia, seeing Running Antelope failing in his mission, ran over and began screaming at the men for being cowards, but her words made no sense to them because she was a woman. And what did she know about being brave or a coward for that matter? If a man had called them cowards, they would have killed him on the spot and buried him under an orange tree and said the proper prayer and put a cross above him because he was a Christian and because he had had the balls to call them cowards. It was a special kind of man who could call others cowards, but she was a woman.

Alicia yelled at them with the passion of a woman in love, although she doubted anything could change the obese man's way of thinking.

"Alicia, this is a man's business," one of the men yelled.

"The women pick oranges too, and we have a voice in this," she yelled back.

"Yes!" one of the women cried out, only to be bopped on the head by her husband. None of the other women spoke up.

"Alicia, look around you. We have picked the trees clean. What's the use of having a strike when there is no fruit on the trees? Maybe next year."

"But it was a great pachanga, Running Antelope. We should do it again."

"Pachanga-man. That's what we'll call you. Pachanga-man!"

"Why don't you come picking strawberries with us?"

"I am not a slave!" Running Antelope cried out, "And you'll be slaves forever!" he continued.

"Let's go," the men said.

"Let's go," the women agreed.

"Let's go," the children followed.

The trucks and cars left in a convoy, leaving a trail of dust behind them. The trees looked bare without their fruit that was now packed and being shipped across the country to be enjoyed by the people who could afford to pay for these freshly picked oranges. But would they know that this fruit had cost the lives of ten sheep and the pride of one man who couldn't understand that food was more important than anything Karl ever said. The fires were still smoldering. Yellow Rose stood by her son and spoke as a mother usually speaks if love is the center of their relationship. She told him to forget lofty ideals for other men. There was nothing he could do to help humanity. Men and women must find their own selves and be happy with what they create. She and Pale Moon were going to pick strawberries. After that they were off to the spinach and cotton fields. Maybe he should join them in the fields and graze peacefully by their side.

"I am not an animal!" he cried out in pain. "I am a man! A human being, Mama!"

"Am I an animal? Is your sister an animal? We must work to eat!"

"It hurts me to see you like this, Mama. I promised father on his deathbed that I would take care of you, but I have failed."

"Practice law, my son. You could help our people then."

"Law is for thieves. I would rather steal the fat man's sheep and cows and remain honest instead of being a thieving lawyer."

"You know best."

Yellow Rose embraced her son and joined the other women. Pale Moon kissed her brother and Alicia and whispered in her ear, "Stay with my brother. He needs you right now."

Alicia and Running Antelope remained in the orchard for a few hours. He sat silently in the shade, mumbling to himself that men couldn't be trusted to change history. Alicia looked at the trees empty of fruit, wondering what life had to offer.

"What shall we do?" she asked.

This question puzzled Running Antelope, perhaps because he was supposed to think about her now.

"Well, we can't stay here!" he said somewhat disgusted as if she had been the cause for his failure.

They walked out of the orchard and took the road that led into town. The road was lined with fields of strawberries with familiar heads and bodies squatting near plants. They were fill-

S. Leconte

ing up baskets with this red fruit, which Alicia had never tasted. For some unusual reason there were several men with shotguns on both sides of the road, and she couldn't understand why men should be guarding strawberries. Running Antelope told her to keep her head straight and not to look at the strawberries. Even a look at the forbidden fruit was a crime punishable by death. There were several signs that warned the workers and passers-by not to look at the fruit that belonged to another obese man, who happened to be the obese man's brother.

According to Running Antelope, several fruit-pickers had been shot, but not to death, for accidentally looking at the obese man's brother's strawberries. The criminals were then brought to justice in front of the obese man's porch where he sat in his rocking chair. The "thieves" (after all, they had coveted the fruit by simply looking at it) stood bewildered. Running Antelope had seen how the poor men begged for their lives as the obese man's brother read from the Bible, "Thou shall not covet thy neighbor's strawberries."

The pickers were confused. Being from across the river, they couldn't understand words like "covet." A translator as white as snow told them not to steal the "fuckin'" strawberries because the Bible the obese man's brother was holding said so!

"We didn' steal no strawberries, señor!"

"You looked at 'em. Just as bad as stealin'!"

"But how are we supposed to pick them if we can't look?"

"By feel, boy. This time you just get shot in the arm. Next time you'll either hang or be shot. Read the signs! Cain't you people read?"

"Sí, señor, but your signs are in English."

"Lemme shoot him now, C.J."

127

"We cain't act like criminals. The man's just tryin' to tell us we ought to have the signs in their *Spinach* language. And suppose I had the signs made in *Spinach*, do you think you people would quit covetin' my strawberries?"

"Then everybody would understand, except those who can't read."

"So what's the use of puttin' up the signs in *Spinach* if most of you cain't read? Just tell your people to look up at the sky when they pick my strawberries."

"Sí, señor."

Alicia couldn't believe that someone would shoot her for picking a simple strawberry out of a field that was abundant with this fruit, but she wasn't about to challenge the men with shotguns who seemed eager to shoot anyone just because they had the guns, and men with guns must shoot something or someone. Otherwise they wouldn't be holding guns. She saw Yellow Rose and Pale Moon bent over plants, picking the forbidden fruit. She called out to them, but they didn't answer. Running Antelope told her to keep quiet until they reached the city limits where the strawberries stopped growing.

When they reached town, Alicia had had time to think Running Antelope's story over. The Bible said nothing about stealing strawberries. Maybe Running Antelope had made it up to frighten her. Then she heard a shotgun blast resound in the distance. She didn't turn around.

In town, Running Antelope told her he had come here to see his sister Morning Star and not to be surprised by what she would see. When they reached the block where his sister worked, night had begun to fall. The air seemed heavier in town, and Alicia was thirsty from not having had anything to drink all day. She also needed to rest her feet. Running Antelope appeared short with her, but he stopped long enough to get her a soda pop. The coolness of the drink ran down her throat like an icy rivulet, and she wanted more, but said nothing.

The street where his sister worked was lined with semi-nude women who showed their bodies to men who drove by and picked them out of the street like strawberries in a human field. Alicia had never seen such women in her life. They were colorful like butterflies and insects, with emerald bodies and hair on fire from the neon lights that bounced against it. Most of the women smoked. She had only seen one woman smoke in her entire life, and she had been a gringa tourist who had gotten lost.

Running Antelope put Alicia on a bench, told her not to move from her spot and ran across the street. He went from woman to woman asking where his sister might be. He ran back and sat down next to Alicia in the silence that seemed to absorb him most of the time.

"What are these women doing here?"

"They sell their bodies."

"How can you sell your body?"

"Alicia, what planet did you come from?"

"Why are you angry at me? Can't you tell me how these women can sell their bodies?"

"My sister is a hooker!!"

"What is a hooker?"

"A puta!"

"What does a puta do?"

"She fucks people for money!"

"Why does your sister do that?"

"Because she hates picking fruit."

"Does she like fucking?"

"Don't say that word like that!"

"Like what?"

"It is to be used in anger. You said it gently. It lacks the punch to it."

"I won't say it again."

"My sister hates it, but she does it to help me and my sister Pale Moon."

"I don't think I could sell my body to any man."

"My sister is a good-hearted person, Alicia. You don't know what you might do to eat one day."

"I don't think I would sell my body."

"Men buy women in various ways. Some give them money. Others marry them and for that give them a house out in the country. The world is short on principles these days, Alicia. Even the president of this country is a puta! He lies to himself to make himself look good. That is worse than being a prostitute."

"My sister, at least, is honest!"

"Running Antelope, what would you do if I sold my body to eat?"

"Why do you ask such questions?"

"To know."

"Know what?"

"Why do you get so angry at me?"

"Because I don't know if I want you."

"You don't love me, do you?"

"Alicia, if you sold your body to another man, I wouldn't kill myself. Is that what you want to hear? First you tell me you could never sell yourself. Now you ask me how I would feel if you did. I would feel like shit! And I would leave you to your men!"

"You didn't abandon your sister."

"She's my sister. You're not!"

"What am I then?"

"You're somebody special, Alicia, but don't ask me to marry you. I have a goal in life."

"I am not asking you to marry me. All I want to know is how you feel about me."

"I have to go at my goal alone, Alicia. I can't be worrying about another person, and I don't want you to worry about me."

"I don't want to worry about you."

"That's good!"

Alicia watched Running Antelope rush across the street where a tall Indian woman with black hair came out of a large white car that reminded her of a sailing boat she had seen in a magazine ad. Running Antelope's sister was wearing a short skirt that showed her legs—legs that reminded Alicia's of a burro's legs, skinny and brown. Her breasts were stuffed in a white shirt that blinked like a chameleon, changing from green to red to blue. As she noticed them speaking, she wondered if he would bring her over and introduce his sister to her. Then she noticed a thin man with glasses approach one of the women. She was wearing a bikini top and laughing as she waved the thin man away. He didn't get angry. Alicia suddenly recognized him as the man of God who had read his messages from his pulpit to the obese man and his thin wife. The minister had come to buy a woman's body. Alicia didn't, however, find it strange, as she recalled Father Romero who had fathered many children back in her village.

The thin minister with glasses spoke to another woman and was laughed at again. Running Antelope ran across the street to rejoin Alicia as the thin man disappeared with Morning Star. Alicia mentioned the minister who had spoken against the pleasures of the flesh. The more she spoke about him the more she remembered the gist of his sermons.

"It is the white man's way. They are hypocrites because they can't accept their own nature. The body has needs and so does the spirit. All the white man does is try to deny both, and he remains incomplete, just a lie to his own reflection in the mirror."

As they walked away from this block, Running Antelope offered to take Alicia out for a hamburger with the money he had gotten from his sister. Alicia was hungry, very hungry, but she couldn't see eating a hamburger with money his sister had earned with her body. It would seem that she, too, had bought a part of her body. How could Running Antelope take money from his sister?

"Aren't you hungry?"

"Yes, but I don't want to be a prostitute."

"Nobody's asking you to be one."

"But you eat with your sister's money. That must make you a prostitute too."

"Yes, I am! And so is the minister and the president and the government because they take taxes from these women. They take money from dope traffickers, alcohol, cigarettes, and they want to remain pure. These women out here don't pretend to be pure. That's why men hate them. That's why men need them. It's here that they come to purify themselves. My sister is pure. So don't be ashamed, Alicia. She would feel respected if you ate a hamburger in her name."

"If you put it that way, then I accept. Running Antelope, could you buy me one strawberry to taste, just to taste?"

"I'll get you a whole basket."

As they were about to enter a supermarket, Alicia saw a young woman who looked like her sister. She called out her name, and the young woman turned around. Her face was made up with loud green and red, her body exposed to lure men like bait floating in the night ocean. Alicia recognized her squirrel-like upper lip and ran into her arms and held her tight against her body, afraid that if she let go, she would lose a part of herself. They both had tears in their eyes. Her sister's make-up melted under the tears. When they stopped crying, her sister Rosa asked her if she had eaten. Alicia introduced Running Antelope. She then told Rosa they were about to buy some strawberries. Rosa smiled and pulled a basket of red juicy strawberries from her purse. Alicia took one, bit into it, and slowly ate it until she savored each little piece. Although she had promised herself to eat only one, she asked if she could have a second. Rosa told her to keep the whole basket, which she did.

Rosa gave her the address where she lived and disappeared into a black beetle-like car. Running Antelope and Alicia went out for a hamburger.

-12-

What Does a Strawberry Really Taste Like?

Alicia and Running Antelope entered Rosa's room like thieves expecting the owner to be home. The light revealed a world of disarray. Rosa hadn't changed, Alicia thought to herself as she noticed clothes strewn all over the floor and furniture, but she had a lot more clothes than she had had at home. The kitchen, which was located in the living room and bedroom, had no dishes or pots. Rosa apparently either ate out a lot or she was fed by the men who took her out. Above the bed Alicia noticed the crucifix that Rosa had taken from her aunt, thinking perhaps that He would save her when she was a girl. Rosa had not given up on the Savior as Alicia had, and she expected another miracle in her lifetime.

Running Antelope mentioned how stifling it was in the room where the roaches scurried from corner to corner in search of food among the crumbs and dust on the worn-out carpet which displayed a now-faceless cowboy sitting on a worn-down nag near a mountain range whose snows had melted long ago. Running Antelope opened the window, letting in a police siren along with the usual night voices of men and women who seemed to have been arguing since the cave days like cats and dogs disagreeing on everything, including the price of sex.

Alicia shook the bedspread and a hundred roaches, the best and biggest since they were from Texas, flew out like fighter planes only to land on the ceiling and kitchen sink where remnants of food seemed to have been splattered especially for them to taste. Tomato sauce and dried pepperoni hung on the ceiling as a symbol of another argument between man and woman. Alicia grabbed the broom and in a fit of anger and frustration began beating the floor with it, smashing and sweeping the dead shells of roaches. She beat the walls and smashed more of their bodies. She beat Christ on the face where a large Texan roach had made its home. She would have continued beating Christ to a pulp if Running Antelope hadn't stopped her.

Alicia was crying out of control. Running Antelope couldn't understand why she was crying. He had bought her a hamburger and a chocolate sundae. She had eaten a pint of strawberries, and she had a place to stay. She had even located her lost sister. To Running Antelope these should have been happy moments. When he asked her what was wrong, she told him that he wouldn't understand.

"Why is it that when men ask women what's wrong, they always answer, 'You wouldn't understand!?'"

"And you think everything should be all right because you bought me one hamburger. I need more than food. I need more than Christ even. And here I am with my sister, and I am sad because she has to do what she does to eat. I don't want her to sell her body to men."

"I understand."

"You don't understand. You can only care about yourself, Running Antelope. You have your goals and ideals, and you want a woman by your side to share those ideals. I am not that woman, but I don't want to be like my sister."

"So do you plan to become a career woman?"

"You make it sound like I am something cheap because I want my own dream!"

"And what is your dream, Alicia?"

"To find a millionaire!" she yelled. "And you're not a millionaire and you're interfering with my dream. You're not capable of loving, are you? Why can't you say, 'I love you?'"

"Because I couldn't love a woman married to a millionaire."

"You couldn't love a poor one either. And why are you too proud to get a job? Why do you feed off your sister? Doesn't that make you a prostitute too?"

"I already said that! And who are you to talk to me like that? I love my sister."

"Then do something about it!"

"Don't tell me what to do!"

Running Antelope ran out the door, leaving Alicia to new tears streaming down her cheeks as if a dam had broken within her. She wondered what she was doing here. She should have stayed at home with her mother and perhaps married José, who was surely pining for her. She suddenly felt sorry for him, but if she had married him, she knew she would have had a miserable life. She couldn't marry out of boredom and despair. Alicia found the room disgusting. How could her sister live in such filth? How could she give herself to just any man? Rosa apparently had not read the pulp romances her sister had. Alicia had wanted one man to love for life ever since she had been a young girl, but this man had to be someone special. He had to love her and be loyal to her, only her. He had to prove his love by deeds and not just words. Flowers would be nice, but she could pick these herself.

There had to be something romantic in her life before she could give herself to a man. Sex that her sister and other girls in the village had experienced was not anything romantic to her. Sex was empty, a means of barter. Unlike most girls, Rosa didn't hate men or try to make men pay for what the fathers had done to their daughters. Rosa kept telling Alicia that sex was like eating or going to the bathroom and something very natural. It was unnatural to spend one's life with one man until you died. There had to be adventure to keep her alive. One man for a lifetime would have killed Rosa. She wasn't looking for love because she was certain it didn't exist. Alicia, on the other hand, believed in love but had a hard time finding any man who would admit that he truly loved her.

Unfortunately for the young men who had courted Alicia, they were unaware that she had been reading romance novels not written in the twentieth century but in the Middle Ages when men were supposed to go on quests to prove their love and manhood to the demanding ladies who waited with impatience for their lovers' return.

Running Antelope came the closest to her idea of a man, but there seemed to be no real deed for him to perform to prove his heroic potential. He had tried to organize a strike with a bunch of cowards and dreams, and he ended up a fool. He had proven to her that he was capable of stealing sheep. Alicia could still taste the garlicky lamb of God in her mouth. At least he would be able to provide for her, but what would happen after he stole all of the obese man's sheep? Although she had objected to his educated talk and especially Karl's economic theories when life was and should be simple, Alicia missed him and he had only been gone less than an hour according to the red numbers on Rosa's clock. She missed hearing the words that had caused her frustration. She missed Running Antelope's frowning brow, which she wanted to smooth with love and her caring touch. She missed his stern stare into the distance as she wondered where he was drifting. But she wouldn't miss him if he were gone forever! There was no sense missing him if he had left without a word. She would dismiss him as she had José and wipe her mind clean. There were other men in this world, and one of them was bound to live up to the image imprinted in her mind. He would be a hero, a millionaire, and he would love her for who she was— Alicia!

As she drifted into a world where men stood in a large marketplace where they were being auctioned off, she heard someone come up the stairs. She was ready to throw herself at Running Antelope and to apologize for reasons unknown to her. Rosa entered the room with several pints of strawberries. There was a serious look on Rosa's face as she went to the sink and washed the fruit. Alicia felt uncomfortable and unwelcome.

"Do you want me to go, Rosa?"

"What makes you say such a stupid thing?"

"I don't know. We know each other pretty well."

"Where's the guy who was with you?"

"He's gone."

"Where did you find an Indian? You always pick losers for men. Ever since you were a girl, the boys were poor. They had nothing to give you but dreams. Do you remember how we used to lie in bed and you would tell me how you dreamed of getting a man who would come and take you away on a big white stallion, and he would be wearing a big sombrero and two pearl-handled guns. He would take you to his camp where you and him would lead the people to a new revolution? You and Pancho would take the land away from the rich and give it to the poor. I really admired your views, Alicia, but I was small then. I didn't understand that nothing changes. There are always the poor and the rich. The poor stay where they are and dream of being the rich people they'll never be or you take your bitching life by the throat and get what you want!"

"Are you happy?" Alicia asked as Rosa sat down next to her and put a strawberry into Alicia's mouth.

"Was I ever happy? Do you remember how we used to look at that picture of a strawberry and say that we would one day taste a real one?"

"Yes, but this strawberry is bitter, Rosa."

"Why is it that you can only see the negative? I am not unhappy."

"Don't you feel ashamed?"

"Who is there to make me feel that way? You? Don't judge me, Alicia!"

"I'm not."

"You are!"

"Why don't you come to work in the fields with me? At least it's honest work, Rosa."

"And what's dishonest about my work? When I was a girl I used to practically give my body away to the young men for nothing. Then I learned how stupid men can be. They want this ass so bad, they would die to get it. Now they pay me! I worked in the fields at first, and I picked oranges and strawberries, but I made barely enough to eat. But the men wanted me. One even raped me! I figured why pick fruit when I can take them and their money?"

"Why do you live in this place, Rosa?"

"Because even now I am a slave to the pimp that robs us, but this is better than picking strawberries."

"Rosa, won't you come with me?"

"And to where? Where, Alicia? You used to run away so many times when you were a girl, but you'd come back and say there was no place to go to. There's no place to run to, Alicia. There's the here and now."

"But you'll never get anywhere here, Rosa. You'll get old."

"Maybe I'll have kids who love me. Maybe a man will come along and take me to his ranch!"

"Maybe, Rosa. I hope so. You know I love you. And there's always Mamá."

"I would die of boredom at home. What's there for any of us anyway, Alicia?"

"It's home."

"So how come you came across?"

"Mamá wants me to find a millionaire."

Rosa laughed as she heard Alicia's reason for coming across and told her that she would never find a millionaire, looking the way she did.

In the morning Alicia rose from the bed, trying not to awaken Rosa, who was sleeping like an angel with pouting lips the color of strawberry juice. She was snorting like a piglet and whispering a name Alicia understood to be Kyle. As she heard his name, she felt a sense of repulsion as she imagined him entering her sister as the stallion entered mares on his ranch. Alicia walked out on the stairs to get a breath of morning air, and a deep sense of solitude suddenly filled her heart. Where was Running Antelope? As she turned around to go back in, she noticed an envelope taped to the door. She noticed her name on it. She tore through it as if it held the secret to her life.

Dear Alicia,

I have decided to go on alone even though I love you. I am sure that you will find someone else to love. It is easy

to do in this day and age. You are a most beautiful woman and you should have no problem finding a millionaire whose heart is in need of love.
Running Antelope
P.S. Take care. It's a cruel world.

Alicia crumpled the note up and like a lost child, began weeping for the man who was being cold towards her. She couldn't wish him ill as most women do in such situations, but she couldn't wish him luck either. She wished he had asked her to go along with him to build the Utopia (a word he had taught her) he had read about. She had dreamed of a giant forest filled with exotic flowers and animals where everything lived in harmony. There were meadows with cattle, sheep and goats herded by small children. The men and women worked in gardens abundant with fruits and vegetables known and unknown. The men and women didn't argue as they did on earth because they ate what they grew themselves. She imagined her mother, her sister Rosa and her brother Rosario working by her side. In the evening the men and women would gather by the river that flowed through Utopia and drink wine made from grapes they grew and tell stories that were pleasant. Running Antelope had painted such a picture of Utopia that Alicia would never be able to erase it from her dreams.

Her tears eventually dried up, and she felt the anger she had to feel in order to kill the love that could not blossom. She wouldn't allow the seed of love to sprout because Running Antelope was just another man rushing after ghosts. He was just another man trying to find windmills to fight like that fool Don Quixote, which she had read and loved until she met Running Antelope and realized that fictional characters are better left between pages and not brought to life. The more she thought about the poor blind fool who needed glasses to figure out his surroundings, she decided that she herself had been foolish for reading books that had misled her and dropped her into this abyss. Running Antelope was probably sitting in the desert alone, like Christ, waiting for a message from above that would never come even if he thought he was holy and had a message for the world. Who was he to impose his view on those around him when he didn't know what was going on in his own heart?

Rosa rose from her bed and stumbled like a butterfly beaten by the wind up to the stove and boiled some coffee. Alicia noticed how pale she had gotten since she had left the village, but she said nothing. She knew how upset Rosa could get when she was critical of her wrongdoings, but Alicia was not the type who could hold her feelings in. Rosa came out on the porch and sat down next to Alicia. She plopped her buttocks down like an old woman tired of life and said, "Alicia, what are your plans?"

"I just arrived, Rosa."

"You should think about getting a job. Maybe I could talk to Pedro, and he could fix you up."

"Doing what?" Alicia asked, frightened by her sister's prospects for her future.

"Look, it's not so bad. We get used to it, and there is money. And this will give you the chance to meet your millionaire."

"I don't want to do what you do, Rosa."

"So now you think you're better than me, is that it?"

"I didn't say that!"

"Even as a girl you thought you were better than me. You just sat there listening to those tapes. You are a dreamer, Alicia. Hope will get you nowhere if you don't make it happen. This is America. You make whatever you want of yourself!"

"Don't you know about the diseases you might get, Rosa?"

"You were always afraid to take chances! You'll never get anywhere thinking about security. It's okay for you to talk, Alicia. You eat my strawberries and live in my room because you don't have to sell your ass!"

"Don't talk to me like that, Rosa. You are supposed to be my sister. I thought you were my sister, but maybe you forgot who you were when you crossed the river. Maybe you'll be my sister again once you go back across."

"I like it in America. What the hell do you think is back home? Frijoles and tortillas? Get married, have kids and get beat up by some drunk husband?"

"But men beat you here!"

"At least I get paid for it."

"And this Pedro steals your money."

"He protects me!"

"By slapping you? I saw this gorilla yesterday and how he slapped you, Rosa!"

The gorilla was short and squatty. His hair was black as coal and long. His face was bearded and his arms were covered with what looked like thousands of spider webs waiting for victims. The gorilla named Pedro wore a fedora hat with a large eagle feather and from his earlobes hung two miniature parrots, one blue, the other green. When he saw Alicia for the first time, his eyes glowed red, and Alicia was certain he was the devil come to tempt her with the material goods of this world. His lips were greasy from the chicken he always ate when he came into Rosa's room to collect his protection money.

"You're a fine looking woman, Alicia. Your sister mentioned to me that you needed a job, but were the shy type. You got nothing to lose here. You could make a lot of money if you hang around with me. You'll find I'm a reasonable man. You could be my woman, and I would find you men who could pay to just touch you. They would be touching a goddess."

"You are filth!" Alicia yelled spitting in his face.

The gorilla left smiling.

The gorilla returned daily to collect his dues and to beat Rosa, whose face sometimes looked like a bruised apple, which she covered with make-up. The dark of night would protect her looks. Besides, men weren't looking for perfect faces. The gorilla let Rosa know that if her sister didn't join his stable, she wouldn't live to see her next birthday. Rosa pleaded with Alicia, but Alicia had principles. She was saving herself for the right man in spite of her lack of religious belief. Rosa asked her what was more important, her sister's life or her virginity? Alicia would have to think about that question.

"You have a choice, Rosa."

"Why is it always my choice when it involves you too?"

"I am not involved, Rosa! You can quit this business and come with me!"

"I don't want to go with you, Alicia. Your damned honesty makes me want to throw up."

"I don't need to stay here. You're not my sister, Rosa."

"You eat my food and most of my strawberries. Why can't you at least leave me my strawberries? I buy them with my own money, but you eat them all. What gives you the right to eat all of them? If you want them, buy them!"

"I don't want your strawberries."

"I can't stand you, Alicia! You never had compassion for anyone."

"And you do because you are killing yourself? You're sorry for the poor because you are abused by men, is that it?"

"I love the poor."

"In your dreams, Rosa. What are you doing to help Mamá?"

"I can't even help myself."

"I know that, Rosa."

"Please, help me, Alicia."

Alicia Maravilla

Alicia couldn't dress up the part of whore to help her sister. The short skirt made of black leather, the see-through blouse, and the high-heeled shoes remained uninhabited, although she had tried them on to see what she would look like. As she had stood in the outfit in front of the mirror, she had at first felt the shame of being naked before other people, but the shame of being without clothes also gave her the pleasure of seeing men begging to take her out. Being naked before the mirror, she understood that men were like children seeking the comfort of her breasts and her vagina. The price they would pay to touch and ejaculate their fears, lack of love, grief, and anger inside her couldn't pay for the loss of pride and honor that she had bred for herself out of the legends she had read like a bird avid for the nectar of the cactus flower. She removed her naked body from her own eyes and threw Rosa's outfit on the bed, cursing the gorilla all the while. She put on the same old dress she had been wearing when she crossed the river and walked out of her sister's room into the street.

-13-

The Love of Christ Can Save You, Alicia

Alicia walked into the night of harsh perfumes on a street where the women paraded their bodies like female lizards exposing their cloacas to men. As she walked from woman to woman in search of Rosa's face that was made up like a mask for the next performance, Alicia didn't know why she was looking for Rosa, except perhaps to say good-bye out of politeness and to make sure her own conscience was clean. As she made her way through the maze of made-up faces, she realized that the Rosa here was not her sister any longer. She had become harsh, cynical, and selfish. How could Rosa begrudge her the strawberries she had eaten? Her sister had really drowned at the river-crossing and been washed away with the clay and silt and would be found in months. This Rosa looked like her sister, except that some strange animal had taken over her body and was making her act like one of the devil bitches sent here from Hell to torment men with their bodies.

Alicia, who had abandoned the church and its beliefs, couldn't help but believe that Rosa and the women who sold their bodies for money and strawberries were possessed by evil lizards that roamed the desert. She was certain that the devil made the women eat these lizards that now inhabited their bodies. Even as she spoke Rosa's tongue had been forked. It was not a human tongue. As she walked from face to face, Alicia paid special attention to the women's mouths as they spoke to the men. She was certain their tongues were viper-like. It was with these tongues that they infected men. They let them slither into men's throats until they could sting their souls with venom. Alicia imagined Rosa's tongue biting through men's skins. Rosa appeared covered with slime, and Alicia was frightened by the absence of the sister she once knew.

Rosa was nowhere to be seen. Their reunion had been short and devoid of the pleasant conversations they had once shared. Alicia and Rosa had been separated by the river they had crossed. Rosa could no longer be called Rosa. She must have forgotten to repeat her own name while crossing the river. Rosa could no longer be her sister, and Alicia wanted to tell her so. Her sister Rosa would not have sold herself to strangers for money. Her sister Rosa would have sent her mother money. She would have written home. Her sister Rosa loved Rosario, and she wouldn't have forgotten his birthday. Where was her sister Rosa? Where was the woman who called herself Rosa and pretended to be her sister? Just because she had Rosa's name didn't make her Rosa.

The lizard women stuck their tongues out and yelled obscenities at some of the men. Smoke escaped from their mouths. Alicia bumped against one of the naked bodies, and the lizard woman lit up with anger.

"Watch where you're goin', sister!"

"I am not your sister!" Alicia spoke up, unafraid of the creature spitting smoke and slime at her.

The lizard woman's face puffed up red and was about to explode. Alicia quickly withdrew, afraid that her touch would infect her and that she might die from the infection or that the infection would cause her to drop her clothes into the street and she would become one of them. She had had a dream that had bothered her. This dream had recurred for several nights while at Rosa's apartment. In this dream Alicia was completely naked and walking on a street similar to the one she was walking on now. In spite of her nakedness, the lizard women didn't believe she was one of them. They called her a traitor to her sex and ran after her. They caught her and held her down, calling her dirty names because she thought she was better than them. Then they tied her to the ground and splayed her legs, leaving her sex exposed to the men who raped her one by one while the lizard women applauded. She was disturbed by the violence she read in the lizard women's faces.

Rosa's face had become hewn by violent hands. Alicia imagined these men eating pieces of Rosa's flesh and turning into lizards themselves. There was no freeing her from the lizard world she now lived in.

Alicia was lost among the lizard women who snapped at her for being on their street. This was their territory, and they had sprayed their female perfume like dogs piss along the walls. They yelled at her, and some were ready to bite her with their rotting teeth. She yelled back and told them how ugly they were because of their evil ways.

"What are you?"

"A Jehovah's Witness?"

"Maybe she's looking for a good time. Lisa, you lick women! Hey honey, go with Lisa. She's got a golden tongue!"

"Stay away from me!" Alicia yelled as she saw them extend their painted claws.

"What have you done to my sister?" she added and then ran across the street, afraid they would follow and tear her flesh like vultures eager to open her belly and eat her intestines.

Thinking herself safe across the street, she watched the lizard women being driven away in cars owned by men with insect-like faces. She imagined them on filthy linen sheets covered with blood from their own lovemaking. They tumbled and tore at each other's flesh, ripping through old wounds to remind one another that this was life. She imagined a bed where Rosa was biting through a man as his limbs flailed to be free from the pain she was inflicting on him.

Alicia suddenly recalled Rosa coming home one night and crying because several young men had raped her. Rosa had said nothing to her mother for fear of causing her mother pain, but she told Alicia, who was then twelve, that men were just cruel and that they took what they wanted. That night at the age of fourteen, Rosa vowed to get what she wanted from them. She would make them pay. But Rosa was fooling herself. She was still paying and there would be no end to it all.

When she lay in bed with Rosa in her arms, trying to soothe the pain away, she felt a hand grab her by her dress and pull her out of the past that made the present unchanged. She turned around to face her assailant. He was a short man with claws for hands. His face was one ugly mask of blame—drunken blame that ejected curses at women. He raised his claws above her head and yelled that he had lost both of his hands during the war and that the bitch had left him for a rodeo cowboy before he could come home.

"And it's your fault, girl!"

The claws grabbed her by the shoulders, and the mask of drunken blame brought her face to his. The more she pulled her head away, the harder the claws held on. He kissed her lips and then pinched her breasts. She cried out in pain as the man, no longer human, turned into a ferocious animal in need of fresh meat to appease his hunger. She yelled for help, but none of the men nearby stepped forward.

"Let him have his fun."

"The man was made loco by the war."

"And his wife left him. Women are such bitches!"

"My wife used to beat me."

"That's because you're a gringo and a pendejo. You should have beat your wife. They deserve a beating a day, man. If you don't beat them they'll get a big head. My wife died, but not because I beat her. She couldn't stand life. So she killed herself. Give it to her, Vet Man!"

"Yeah, give it to her!"

"Fuck her, man. We wanna see you fuck her!"

The men quickly turned into coyotes, their teeth drawn like knives, ready to eat her flesh raw. Alicia beat the man in the face, drawing blood from his eyes. The mask of drunken blame cried out in pain and yelled more obscenities at women. Alicia moved away from the crowd of men, holding on to her tattered dress and wounds, like an animal being hunted down because of hatred. The men comforted the mask of blame that demanded that she be killed for doing what she had done.

"He could be blind! Look what you did to him!"

"She blinded a man who served his country!"

"You blinded a hero, bitch!"

Alicia ran across the street, thinking the women would protect her from the men, but these women took the Vet's side and blamed her for not being a good sport. One of the lizard women pushed her and Alicia fell against the pavement, hurting her knees. She knelt long enough to catch her breath and consider the bare legs before her face. Alicia looked up from below and saw the dark-haired iguana in a green shirt, chewing gum and spitting at her.

"You are scum. Why do you come on our street? You should fuck that Vet and then we might forgive you."

"I don't want any trouble."

Alicia Maravilla

"You caused it, honey! Now get off this street before we hand you over to the coyotes. They do love fresh meat, especially virgin meat."

Alicia got up on her feet and hobbled away in pain, frightened for her life. She couldn't understand why these people should want to hurt her when she had done nothing to them. As she moved away from the lizard women, she heard Rosa call out her name. Alicia turned around and saw her get out of a car. The minister of the Baptist Church was at the wheel. Alicia waited until the car drove off to approach Rosa.

"The man needs my ass more than he needs God, Alicia. So what are you doing out here? Trying out the streets? I'm glad you changed your mind, but you won't get men to pick you up with the dress you're wearing."

"I didn't change my mind. I came looking for you to tell you I can't stay with you. I feel guilty eating your strawberries. I can't take food that belongs to you because you're not my sister. My Rosa died when she crossed the river and put her foot on the other shore. You are not Rosa! Good-bye and thank you for the use of your room."

"Alicia, please, you don't understand!" Rosa yelled as Alicia walked away into the dark of night, leaving the ghost of Rosa who used to be her sister. Rosa was now at the mercy of the lizard women and coyotes that roamed this desert of streets in search of fresh meat and blood.

As she imagined coyotes howling and hacking at the lizard women with knives and machetes to seek revenge against the females of this world for having nurtured them, Alicia heard sirens in the back of her. Red and blue lights bounced against the sky. It looked and sounded like a strange animal crying because of wounds. Alicia returned to the street where Rosa might awaken. As she reached the street, men in black uniforms were rushing like black beetles with clubs that came

152

crashing against the lizard women's backs. The coyotes remained on their side of the street and watched. Alicia noticed Rosa being dragged towards a van.

"Rosa!" she cried out as if wounded herself. Alicia ran up to Rosa, her sister, now that she was bleeding and begging to be free. The black beetles pushed Alicia away and told her to watch it or she'd get the same.

"We got our own hookers! We don't need no river rats to give us diseases!" one of the beetles spat out of his mouth.

"Rosa, please, go home!"

"Don't worry, Alicia. They will take me across. You watch out for yourself."

"I will!"

As the van drove off, Alicia's heart realized how awful she had been to her sister in the past. She somehow felt that Rosa would not remain on the other side of the river. She would cross it in the night again and find another city with another street and other lizard women and coyotes with whom she would find the comfort of despair and where hope would remain out of her reach. But she would have an endless supply of strawberries, and maybe Rosa had reached her ideal. Maybe her sister had made it in this land where opportunity knocks on strange doors. Rosa had reached the land of strawberries and was happy to taste the fruit that freed her from the desert world. Rosa had never wanted to get married because men were cruel and abusive once they were tied down. Here on the streets she could pick and choose the men that yearned to lick her skin clean with their tongues purified by the need to enter her. Rosa regained her virginity every time she made love.

Alicia despaired that night as she sat in a park, hiding behind bushes like a jackrabbit fearing for its life. She dreamed of home, craving the simple taste of frijoles and tortillas. She yearned to hear her mother's not-so-gentle voice. The villagers appeared to her in a dream. They had grown impatient for her return with the millionaire husband she had promised them. They now stood on the other side of the river. Some were already sticking their feet into the water. She looked at them and cried out for them not to cross because they would regret the crossing. She warned them about obese men with lecherous mouths. She warned them about women so thin that their souls were shriveled, even though they cried out God's name. She told them to care for their children, especially the girls, or the lizard women and coyotes would drag them into the night, devour their souls and leave them as shells they wouldn't recognize as their daughters.

As Alicia warned them, they raised their fists and shook them until a heavy wind rose from their side. She could hear each voice curse her. They were clearly curses.

"You are enjoying life over there, eating roast beef you promised us so many times!" Father Romero yelled at her, holding a crucifix in the air and pointing his head at hers as if to cast a spell against her. He continued to speak, "Alicia, you have been dishonest with our people. They have eaten roast beef and drunk enough wine in their dreams. Now they want the real thing. You cannot promise people what you cannot deliver. Heaven is out of our reach. Roast beef they could smell and taste because the scent of meat comes from the other side when the winds are favorable."

"She's enjoying herself and lying to us!"

"She wants us to keep on starving. She has become a gringa, and she wants us to stay here."

"She found her a millionaire."

"And she doesn't want to share him!"

"She's just like her sister Rosa."

"And her mother."

"They all think they're better than us."

154

"We want our children to have a better life, Alicia. Please, understand."

"Speak for yourself, you pious bitch! I want to eat like a man."

"Me too!"

"Frijoles are for women!"

"Meat! Beef is a real man's food!"

"That's what the gringos eat. Are they better than us?"

"And I have seen their women eat beef too. She was sitting on my television set. Her name was Melinda. ¡Qué linda! And she was opening her mouth. Oh, what a mouth, so red and juicy, and her hands were so pure as she cut the piece of meat and someone said for her, "Meat is a woman's food too!"'"

"Why didn't she say it herself?"

"Gringas don't talk with their mouths full."

"I don't think our women need meat. Look what happened to the gringas once they started eating beef. They started smoking and drinking like men."

"Look what happened to Juan's wife when she ate that whole chicken."

"Did she lay an egg?"

"No, you fool, she cackled for a week and then she laid a dozen eggs and started beating her husband."

"That's what he deserves for marrying a chicken!"

"We want beef, not chicken!"

"We want beef! We want beef!" they all began to chant, including the women. Father Romero led the pack across the river and tried to touch her with the cross. She raised her hands to his head and woke up.

-14-

Popeye, the Sailor Man

With no sister to turn to, Alicia was on her own, moving as quickly out of town as she had come in. At this point she forgot Rosa existed and cursed herself for not having eaten last night's supper. Rosa had developed a taste for Chinese food and had tried to make Alicia like it too because she liked it.

That was logical, and Alicia did not refuse it until she tried the chewy boiled octopus and the hundred-year-old egg that stank so bad Alicia thought her sister had farted. Rosa laughed as Alicia had never seen her laugh. It was a light laughter that made the air bubble and caused her to laugh too.

"Rosa, how do you eat this food? I don't like octopus! Look at these little cups! I read somewhere that octopus suck their victims dry."

"I never read such a thing. Maybe vampires, but not octopus. If it sucked blood, I wouldn't eat it. Did you ever see me eat vampire?"

"No, never. But how can you eat that egg? They bury them until they stink and then sell them to. . . . "

"Alicia, have you ever eaten anything other than tortillas and frijoles?"

"Yes!"

"What? Besides all the strawberries?"

"I had French fries and hamburgers, and we always used to eat chicken on Fridays when we were at home."

"Alicia, that kind of food is shit! Haven't you heard about the cholesterol poison that is infecting the gringos' brains?"

"What's cholesterol?"

"It's a poison that is found in beef, and I bet you all Texan men die of heart attacks. If you're gonna marry anybody, you should marry a Texan. He'll die and leave you all his beef and money. You sell the cattle and move back home."

"Suppose he lives a long time, and I am stuck with a man I don't like, Rosa? Then what?"

"Then you send him to Hell!"

"Rosa!"

"You are thick, Alicia. If he doesn't die on his own, then you feed him beef and sausage until his heart turns to one big chunk of fat."

"That's murder!"

"Alicia, how can you call that murder when you are fulfilling your domestic obligations?"

"I guess I should feed him foods he likes!"

"And Texans love fatty foods, Alicia."

"I don't think I want to marry a Texan, Rosa."

"Well, you are in Texas now, and when in Texas. . . . "

"Maybe I would like to go to New York, Rosa. I hear New York men treat women like countesses."

"You're not living in the sixteenth century, Alicia. Try some of this dog meat. It'll warm your soul."

"Ai chihuahua. . . . Rosa!!"

"And it's not a chihuahua. The cook told me it was pure German shepherd."

"Rosa, what's come over you?"

Alicia reached the strawberry fields by noon. She remembered the signs that warned passers-by of looking straight

ahead and not to covet the obese man's brother's strawberries.
Alicia didn't have to read the signs, since the men with shotguns were enough to trigger her memory of the penalty that
might await her if she even blinked at a strawberry. She carefully stepped up to one of the men with shotguns and asked if
she could begin picking. The man's face was stern, his jaws
shut tight as a clam. Perhaps he had had his tongue cut out by
the obese man's brother for eating one of the strawberries
without paying for it. The man, as tall as a scarecrow, stared at
the workers ahead of him like a hawk ready to pounce on his
prey. Alicia repeated her question. Unable to concentrate
because of her presence, the man with clam jaws pointed to
the only tree in the open space near the house where the obese
man's brother lived. She walked along the edge of the road, her
head held high as if she were carrying a basket of eggs on it. It
took forever to reach the house that seemed so close because
she could see it.

When Alicia reached the house, the obese man's brother
was sucking on crab legs, butter dripping along the edge of his
lips. His wife, as obese as him, sat next to her husband and
sucked on shrimp shells. From time to time she emitted grunts
like a pig approving of the food her husband had provided.

"Theo, this is the sweetest shrimp I ever had."

"Should try these crab legs, honey pie."

Alicia approached slowly but didn't care to go too close to
the porch for fear she might disturb their supper and incite
their wrath for interrupting their stomachs' digestion, but her
presence didn't bother them as she had expected it might. As
a matter of fact, they ignored her image altogether and proceeded to grunt and fart at leisure, which made the obese
woman laugh and snort. The woman's laughter and grunting
made the obese man's brother happy. When they finished the
crab legs and shrimp, they dumped the shells on the ground
where a mangy dog ate what it must have thought was meat.

Once the obese man's brother and woman had eaten, the woman, whose eyes seemed to be hidden in folds of skin, proceeded to lick her husband's lips and face. Alicia saw the woman's hand unzip the obese man's brother's zipper. Alicia turned around and walked away from the scene staged for her.

"Don't walk away mad, darlin'," the obese man's brother yelled.

Alicia continued to walk away. She needed a job, but she was unwilling to watch a man and woman have sexual intercourse like animals without shame. She reached the road, her heart filled with fear as she saw dust rise far in the distance. She hurried across the road that led to other fields. Alicia would find out years later from Pale Moon that the obese man's brother was running a pornography ring that involved several ranches and fruit pickers who were willing to perform acts with dogs and donkeys for the obese man's brother's amusement. He has since become reborn and become senator of his state in Washington, D.C., where he legislates in favor of the little man like himself.

Alicia ran as fast as she could until she reached fields that were not populated by the luscious strawberry, which had caused her sister to sell her body. She suddenly believed that strawberries were the cause for women giving themselves up to men. She had never seen a man eat strawberries and that is why men didn't sell themselves. She had eaten pints of the fruit and realized that her dreams had been of a sexual nature because of what she had eaten. She would never mention them to anyone.

The fields she had come upon were green and leafy with spinach, but the pickers wouldn't arrive for another week or two, giving the plants a chance to mature more. At the entrance of the ranch Alicia noticed a large sign with a sailor, skinny and gangly, flexing one turtle-like muscle. His face looked like a smashed beehive, and he had a pipe stuck in the corner of his mouth. At his feet knelt a thin woman with thin legs and arms, and on her chest was drawn a heart as red as a watermelon. The caption read: "Women still like a strong man. So eat your spinach and be like Popeye the sailor man."

Alicia thought the poster goofy and unbelievable. How could women love a man because he ate spinach? The logic of the caption, of course, escaped Alicia because she had never seen a man eat spinach, but if she had ever seen the Popeye cartoon on television, she would have realized the truth of the statement made on the poster. She would not be seeking a millionaire but a spinach-eating man who would be her hero until she grew disappointed with him. Lucky for Alicia she had not seen any of the Popeye cartoons, and the millionaire remained firmly imbedded in her mind, although she was clearly having doubts: millionaires didn't fall out of every tree as she had been told in her childhood.

As Alicia walked towards a mansion with tall columns, she recalled her mother telling her that if you wanted a lemon, you shook a lemon tree, but first you had to find a lemon tree. She had seen lemon trees in the obese man's orange orchards, and now all she had to find was a millionaire tree where she imagined men hanging by the branches with bags of money she would use to free her village from poverty forever. They would all have money. But suppose they all got a small amount of the million?

And how many coins does a million have? But suppose everyone was a millionaire, and no one grew spinach? It was a frightening thought. But seeing so much greenery around her, Alicia's faith in humanity was quickly restored.

Alicia rang the doorbell and stepped back a safe distance in case another obese man should pop out with some nasty demand. The door opened and a smile, as wide as a river, greeted her. The smile belonged to a tall and thin man in a sailor hat and suit, but his face was gentle and clean-shaven, and he didn't have a pipe in his mouth. The smile stretched his hand out, and Alicia looked at the fingers, long and well manicured, wondering what she should do with the hand. A child brought up to fear strangers, Alicia didn't take the hand for fear the stranger might pull her into the house and never let her out again. The smile vanished from the thin man's face, and Alicia sensed his feelings had gotten hurt. The smile, now a frown with several wrinkles, opened his mouth and said in a very nasal, almost wooden voice, "Oh com'on, it's just a shake."

"I am sorry," Alicia said.

"You're not from around here, are you?" the smile asked slowly.

"No."

"All right, just so that you get it right, I'll close the door again and you ring the bell. Right? And I'll stretch my hand and you shake it."

Alicia rang the bell again, and the wide smile waited the appropriate length of time to answer. The door opened, and he stretched his hand out. Alicia shook it, and the smile smiled an even broader smile. He let go of her hand and told her that there was nothing to be afraid of in this world. He asked her what she wanted, and she told him she was looking for a job picking spinach leaves. Although she had never seen or eaten spinach in her entire life, she had heard of the word and knew what it meant in English. Yet she didn't know what spinach really was. It suddenly dawned on her that words couldn't really be truly understood until they had been tasted and their vowels and consonants thoroughly digested.

The smile vanished and a terribly sad mouth emerged to tell her that spinach season wouldn't start for another week or two, and that he was very sorry to turn her away when she looked so hungry. He wished her luck elsewhere and hoped to see her in his fields when picking time began. As he was about to close the door, a voice quite different from the smile echoed in the house as if it had resonated in the mountains. There was something liquid and loving about the voice as the words seemed to linger like clouds refusing to move on to green pastures. Another smile sneaked out from behind the first smile. This one belonged to a thin woman. Alicia had expected her to be dressed in a sailor suit and to stretch out her hand as her husband had. But she was wearing a business suit Alicia had seen women wear in magazines. The woman rushed out the door as if her house were on fire and grabbed Alicia's body and shook it with her own, hugging her until there wasn't a breath left in Alicia's lungs. She looked at the woman, wondering why she had hugged her when the smile, belonging to the woman, turned serious and her forehead became crumpled like a linen sheet. Alicia heard the woman exclaim in her liquid voice that she had nothing to fear here because they were good people, Methodists, liberal Democrats and of German origin, who unlike the other ranchers, believed in the equality and respect of all mankind with no exceptions.

The woman finished her lengthy speech, which included excerpts from a document called The Constitution. The speech, pronounced with a lawyer's flair, had been spoken with a cold passion and had made Alicia thirsty. All she wanted was a job, and the woman offered her words. The smile on the woman wondered why they were all standing at the door when she had been thinking of calling several of her girlfriends to organize their forces to protect the rattlesnake from extinction.

"So what's going on here, Sam?"

"Vera, she is asking for a job in our fields, and I told her we don't start picking for another week or two."

"Oh, Sam, how could you be so cruel? Of course, we can hire her. We need help with the house. I know you have to keep house for me and cook for me as you did for your mother, but here we have the opportunity of a lifetime, a gift from Heaven if you will, and I think we should hire her. What's your name, dear?"

"Alicia."

"Oh, Sam, did you hear her name, and the way she said it?"

"But Vera, my cooking and cleaning are an expression of my love to you. And how will she know how to make your favorite soufflés?"

While the man's smile was crumbling, the woman was growing like a rainbow after a summer shower. She grabbed Alicia's hand and led her into the house. The air here was cool. The wide rooms and tall ceilings made Alicia feel small and afraid to walk. The woman looked at Alicia's feet, and she looked at hers, thinking it some strange ritual.

"We remove our shoes in this house, Alicia," Sam said. Alicia removed her shoes at the door even though the man and the woman had theirs on.

The woman turned to her husband and asked him to entertain Alicia while she made several phone calls to her friends before the rattlesnake disappeared from the face of the earth. Before leaving Alicia in her husband's hands, the woman had to say a few words about herself and the rattlesnake she was desperately trying to save because it was a creature in God's kingdom. Alicia, hearing the word "God" spoken again, wondered if they too believed in Him with the fervor expressed by others she had met. As the woman spoke, Alicia realized that God's kingdom was just a figure of speech, and as she learned later on, figures of speech didn't mean a lot. They were just words without a bite, without love. Just figures of speech.

The woman explained that she believed in the preservation of species great and small. They, as a family, didn't believe in eating beef, chicken, rabbit or even rattlesnakes, which in this part of country had become part of a culinary cult. The man and the woman with smiles, now frowns that resembled heavy grey clouds, were vegetarians through and through, and they couldn't really understand why people who claimed to be so religious could eat rattlesnakes when snakes were, after all, the symbol of evil. The woman couldn't see how people could consider the snake evil. Alicia listened and thought that perhaps if the woman were bitten by one she would change her mind. The woman thought that men and women who ate rattlesnakes were no better than the rattlesnake. The man and woman, as they mentioned several times during Alicia's stay, were reformed beef-eaters and had at one time eaten rattlesnakes on their barbecue grill, but ever since their spirits had been touched by Popeye and spinach, they had given up their evil ways and were now dedicated to liberal causes and helping the farm workers by paying decent wages and giving them free food—all the spinach they could eat. The woman finished her presentation and expressed how happy she was that Alicia had shown up at their doorstep.

The woman finally went to call her friends before she got carried away by another liberal cause, and left Alicia to Sam who insisted on being called Sam and not Mr. Anything. He, too, believed in many things, and Alicia's ears now listened to what he had to say.

Sam, as he really insisted on being called, believed in spinach, spinach, spinach. Since Alicia had never tried it in her life, it appealed to her taste buds, which were ready to taste anything because she was starving, although she was now wary of what she ate, especially after the dreams she had had just because of the pints of strawberries she had eaten like a sheep let loose on the open prairies. And since the man and woman were giving it away willingly to the workers, she wouldn't mind eating it to truly know the meaning of spinach.

Sam was a little disappointed with the people he tried to help. The workers, when in his fields, didn't steal from him as they did at other ranches that offered melons, oranges, strawberries and other sweet fruits. The workers plain refused to eat his spinach. Alicia couldn't understand why hungry people would refuse to eat spinach but let Sam speak.

"Spinach is life. Spinach is full of iron and vitamin K. It is the essence of life. There's nothing like spinach. My wife Vera and my son Curtis believe that spinach can feed the world. Find me a weak man and a can of spinach will rejuvenate his spirit and body, Alicia. I must say that I am reluctant to let you loose in my kitchen, but Vera is rather impetuous when she feels passionate about people and her beliefs. We are not like the rest of the world. We don't eat meat, period! And we do eat spinach three times a day, but it must be mixed with other foods properly. Curtis doesn't like it plain. We do eat frijoles, but not chile. And we do love tortillas. And if you know how to make them from scratch, you will have gained a niche in our hearts!"

"I don't make tortillas. My mother does, but she buys it from a freezer."

"Oh what a shame! I was looking forward to eating some of your tortillas."

"I don't make tortillas!"

"I am glad you are honest, Alicia. Candid is what you are. Well, since you don't know how to cook . . . "

"Señor, I know how to cook frijoles and make bologna sandwiches."

"Bologna sandwiches?"

"Yes."

"It's meat!"

"These bologna sandwiches are made from shark meat and soya beans. That's what I read in a magazine," Alicia said as she proffered a copy of *Las Americas* in Spanish.

"I believe you, but I don't speak Spanish. Now, I think it's time to educate you. Before we go and show you around you must watch Popeye in action."

Alicia followed Sam into a large room with a gigantic television screen on the wall. She was told to sit down and watch Popeye the sailor man. Sam opened several packages of fresh spinach and made Alicia a spinach sandwich flavored with mayonnaise. While the sailor on the screen was beating up on a fat bearded man named Bluto, Alicia ate her first spinach sandwich, which to her tasted delicious because she hadn't eaten all day. She saw Popeye beaten to a pulp by the fat man. A can of spinach popped out of nowhere like a miracle and the spinach jumped into the sailor's mouth. Revived, Popeye's arms and fists grew like bunions and he bounced Bluto from one corner of the universe to the other. Spinach wasn't bad at all, Alicia concluded.

-15-

More Spinach

A surprised Alicia was given a room next to Curtis in the same house, but his parents were not worried about any goings-on, sexual or otherwise, between the two because their son had received a most proper upbringing in spite of their liberal outlook, which excluded sexual intercourse with the "native" girls, who were either diseased or already pregnant. The parents also objected to the white man's mentality of "screwing" the ethnic minorities of the land or any other land for that matter. Besides, Curtis was engaged to a pretty lily-white-skinned girl, also with liberal views, and who prided herself on her two melon-sized breasts, round buttocks and pearly white teeth that had yet to see a cavity because of the constant brushing and the spinach she ate.

It may appear on the surface that Sam and Vera might have been racists because they wouldn't allow their son to go out with Alicia or any "native" girl, but the person thinking such a thought would have been far from the truth. Sam and Vera believed in the sanctity of spinach and wanted their kingdom to continue after their deaths. Curtis was bound to marry only a spinach-loving girl. Now suppose Alicia loved spinach? Then what? That question may never be answered.

Alicia Maravilla

Alicia's room was comfortable, to say the least. It had its own bathroom with a toilet that had a toilet seat and running water. It also had a white tub. But why would people use water in a toilet? Alicia, who had used the outhouse as a child, was fascinated by the water in the toilet and even more by the shower and the tub, all of which she touched with her hands to feel the smoothness of the white enamel. Alicia thought that if she had a bathroom as clean as this one back home, she would never have left it.

Alicia walked slowly and on tiptoe through the rooms so as not to wake from the dream she must have been having. She looked at herself in the mirror and realized that she was still among the living because she could see herself. She plopped on the bed and its bounciness amazed her. Like a babe smelling flowers for the first time, she stuck her nose in the pillow and took a deep breath of the perfume-like scent. Alicia was in Heaven. And she couldn't believe what she saw before her eyes! Her own television set and a bowl full of fruit: apples, bananas, grapes and one large melon. At first she thought they might be made of plastic to decorate the room as the thin woman had in her living room. Maybe they had been placed there to tempt her soul, and they would vanish before she could touch any of them. She had read about Tantalus, in Spanish, of course, and how he had to undergo cruel and unusual punishment by the gods for teasing them.

Alicia rose from the bed and carefully reached for a banana, which to her surprise remained yellow, whole and real in her hand, but no sooner had she decided on the reality of the fruit she was holding than she heard a knocking at the door. She put the banana back in its place and looked away from it. She opened the door, and Vera asked her if she could come in. Of course, she could. After all, this was her home. Vera explained that as long as she stayed in her home, this room was her room, and anything in it was hers too. These fig-

ures of speech, perhaps expressed out of politeness or out of
Vera's subconscious, caused Alicia to believe that the banana in
the bowl had been a plant to test her honesty. She would never
touch it and would let it rot.

"This fruit was put here for you. We expect to see it gone.
We are not a wasteful people, and we eat everything we have.
And always tell the truth even if the truth hurts. The truth is
what makes our society function. I am a lawyer. I know that
may sound strange to you, but any woman can reach her goal
if she tries. We are here to help you, Alicia. You must have a
goal in life and if we can do anything to help you reach that
goal, we will. Take the banana. I know you're probably starving. Dinner is at six. Now peel it. Don't be afraid. The banana
won't bite you. Haven't you ever had a banana before?"

Alicia shook her head as she chewed on the banana as
politely as she could, trying to tell her hunger to stop behav-
ing like an uncivilized glutton. Vera then asked what her goal
in life might be. Unable to think of any clear aim, she mentioned her mother's dream that she should marry a blue-eyed
millionaire.

"Alicia, you should never marry a man for his money! You
should love him first."

"But señora?"

"Call me Vera."

"But Vera, life is strange. I cannot seem to find a millionaire to love. How do you find a millionaire?"

"In a bank vault counting his millions."

"I don't understand."

"What I'm trying to say is that these millionaires have no
love in their heart, Alicia."

"Your son is nice."

"My son?"

"He is a millionaire, isn't he?"

"Not yet. Please, excuse me!"

Vera disappeared, and Alicia felt free to eat the grapes she had also been tempted with earlier. As she started to pop a grape into her mouth, she felt it must be sour because Vera was now yelling at her son. Alicia, fearing for her own life in these strangers' house, put her ear to the wall and heard what she wished she hadn't heard.

"And stay away from that new girl! I will not have you ruin our reputation!"

Alicia understood Vera from the very beginning, and steered clear of Curtis, who remained polite with the new help and stayed out of her way. Curtis was the perfect gentleman and stayed out of her room, as he had not done with the former help whom he lured into his arms perhaps with these grapes, bananas, and melon. Alicia understood that Vera was the mistress of the house who commanded the ranch, the spinach legacy, and her husband Sam, whose name didn't make him any stronger than he was supposed to be. His parents, as Alicia found out later, had named him after Sam Houston, but this hero's character had not rubbed off on Sam, who was a disappointment to his parents for not living up to their standards. But they had left him as the sole inheritor of this spinach ranch and were amazed before they died that their legacy would survive.

The first few days during her stay at the Popeye Spinach Ranch, Alicia quickly learned that Vera was a topnotch lawyer with a cold edge to her in spite of the smile she offered. This smile frightened her. Alicia knew that beneath it lurked teeth and fangs that could be deadly. She was afraid to leave her fingerprints anywhere, especially after hearing the many stories of convictions and death sentences for those who stole and killed. Vera was a prosecuting attorney and enjoyed retelling trials with the finest of details at the dinner table where Alicia was allowed to sit and listen and listen and listen as Sam and Curtis did out of courtesy and perhaps fear for their own lives.

In a very frightful dream Alicia was reaching for a guava. Just as she touched the green fruit that was still attached to its branch, Vera popped out of the tree with a machete in her hand. Alicia wondered why she had a machete. Vera cried out, like a screeching hawk, that the fruit was not ripe and that she was committing a cardinal sin. The fruit was as green as an innocent child and still had the right to live before it was born to die, but you, Alicia had no right to pick what was not rightfully yours. Vera demanded that Alicia stick her hands out to be cut off. As the machete crunched through her wrists, Alicia opened her eyes and cursed the guava she had grown accustomed to because Vera had praised the fruit for its vitamin content. Alicia vowed not to touch anything that didn't belong to her, which was hard to do since nothing belonged to her, not even the dress on her back. Vera had been kind enough to take Alicia shopping for clothes, which Alicia found to be a delicious experience because of the multitude of choices that could lead any person to madness.

During those first few days, while Vera was at work making sure society was safe from thieves, rapists, murderers, dope-pushers, pornographers, and cheating husbands, Sam took care of Alicia in the most proper way. He opened new avenues into her culinary world where she learned to make spinach soufflés, spinach quiches, spinach ratatouilles, spinach potage, spinach salad, and learned French at the same time. Sam was proud of Alicia, who was not only a good learner, but also a good eater. No sooner had she learned these recipes than she was let loose into the kitchen, and without missing a clove of garlic, a dash of pepper or a teaspoon of salt, she fixed meals that amazed Vera's and Sam's palates. Curtis had developed anti-spinach tendencies, and his parents worried that he would not continue their legacy.

Alicia served the family and then sat down at the same table with them, where she was at first surprised because they allowed one so poor and dark as her to sit with them. The first day she was allowed to sit at their table, she remained mute and solid as marble, afraid to touch the spinach lest it be taken away by the hand that gave willingly. Now that she had spent a week there, all inhibitions were thrown to the wind and Alicia ate not as a guest but as the owners did, and when asked how her day had gone, she was more than willing to relate her adventures in the kitchen.

The days passed quickly in this house, the hours falling off the clock like water off a cuckoo's back, and Alicia thought this place was Heaven. She could eat spinach mixed with potatoes, salads, or soups and never get tired of it. At night while lying alone in her spacious bed, she even noticed that her biceps had grown. One day while there was a lull at the table she stood up out of the blue and flexed her muscles like Popeye had done in cartoons. Sam laughed aloud, finding the scene amusing, and he thought she'd make a great Popeye. His mind rolled out ads with Alicia dressed as a sailor and eating spinach out of a can. There would be a video with Alicia dancing with Popeye the cartoon character. "Oh, how wonderful! You are my savior, Alicia!" Sam exclaimed. Vera didn't find Alicia amusing, and she told him not to make fun of women by making them into caricatures. Vera objected to racism and sexism of any kind. Cartooning people was definitely out! As she left the table she took Alicia with her for a consultation.

"Alicia, I hope you like it here," Vera said as she looked about the room where Alicia slept.

"Yes, Vera."

"That's good. And you are a very clean girl, and your intelligence amazes me. You're not like the rest of the 'native' girls. I would like to see you achieve in this world, and I can help you. How would you like to go to the university I attended?"

"I don't know. I like it here."

"It's not a matter of liking it here. One day you'll have to move on and where will you be? And when we die, what will happen to you, Alicia? I am quite concerned about your future."

"Thank you, señora."

"Vera, dear."

"Thank you, Vera, but you don't plan to die soon, do you?"

"We don't plan to die."

"Then I have nothing to worry about."

"Alicia, you must learn to listen when you are spoken to. You must try to rise above your status or you will remain dirty and poor for the rest of your existence. And what would have happened if it hadn't been for us?"

"I am very grateful to you and Sam."

"Speaking of Sam . . . He is a very nice man but quite misguided."

"I don't think so. He's very nice to me. And he helps me with the spinach. It isn't easy to memorize French, especially when the whole recipe is in French. But he gave me a dictionary and told me to learn it all from scratch, and we sit together and he teaches me."

"That's grand, Alicia, but do you see what I mean by misguided? What man would cause a woman to learn to make quiche from a French cookbook?"

"I don't mind."

"Well, you should! A woman has the right not to learn French! I never learned it, and I refuse to eat anything with a French name!"

"But you ate the ratatouille."

"I barely touched whatever it is you called it."

"Vera, why are you so angry? Were you not pleased with the meal I fixed?"

"The meal was perfect, Alicia. French, however, is not for women like you and me. I have seen these creatures who took French turn into arrogant, self-centered sluts! And Alicia, I would hate for anything of the sort to happen to you. You are not like them. You are a giving person."

"I try to give of myself."

"Just don't you wear any sailor suits. Sam, you see, wanted me to keep him company at home and wear a sailor suit too, but I am my own woman, and I want you to be your woman too! I am glad you are very happy here!"

"Yes, señora."

"Vera."

"Yes, Vera."

After this woman-to-woman talk, Alicia heard nothing more from Sam on the video that might have catapulted her to instant spinach stardom, and he left her to herself in the kitchen with the French dictionary that was supposed to deliver her from ignorance and to the civilized world of culinary renaissance. This knowledge, according to Sam, would bring her out of her misery and erase what memory of poverty she might still harbor. Sam was trying to make a new woman out of her by making her gargle French sounds. They had actually practiced gargling together to get the "r" rrrrrolling in the right direction. But now she was lost between verbs and herbs, adjectives and endives and just made spinach bouillabaisse to please everyone's palate. The meals got worse and worse, and Sam blamed Vera who was happy to be eating the slop Alicia fixed because it contained spinach grown on their land.

She thought she wouldn't be kept around much longer, but to her surprise she was kept on by Vera, whose liberal views on cooking endeared Alicia to her, while Sam would run out and throw up because the meals hadn't been French enough. Sam, not Vera, was first to suggest that he return to the kitchen so that the cooking would return to normal. A fight, not an argument or a spat, ensued, and truth was fleeced, plucked, gutted, and digested until Vera won out and beat Sam the sailor man in spite of the spinach he ate. But then Vera had also eaten spinach all her life, and could beat any of her adversaries in court for it. Sam stayed out of the kitchen, and Alicia was allowed to plod through the dictionary and cookbook and she ruined every meal until Vera herself got sick and thought she was dying of food poisoning, for which she blamed Sam and the French. To remedy the situation, Vera bought Alicia a cookbook written in English (American actually) and Alicia was relieved not to have to search words she couldn't find in the Lilliput dictionary Sam had given her. Yet as she cooked their meals, Alicia felt something missing from the kitchen. She began missing the French words that had tasted as good as the meals. She wished Sam had never abandoned her lessons, but she said nothing and went on, wondering what university life would be like.

When Alicia asked Vera about the university she had attended, she told her that a good mind like hers should not be ruined by an education system that fostered ignorance and prevented people from really thinking. Alicia didn't know what to think. She never mentioned the word university again and let the education she might have gained slip through her fingers. She should never have tried to imagine herself sitting in the French class that was supposed to improve her cooking. The problem with Alicia was the fact that she was voraciously devouring books and magazines, the pages that for the most part remained unturned because Sam and Vera loved them but had no time to read anymore. Curtis never touched these books because he was getting a university education and came home on the weekends to rest his brain from the torture the professors were inflicting on him. Vera was proud of her son because he was her son. Sam hated him because he was his son and because he refused to wear his Popeye the sailor suit.

"I don't want to be a cartoon character, Dad!"

"Are you calling me a cartoon character, is that it?"

"No, Dad. I just don't want to be you. I want to be me!"

"You are me, but you just don't want to wear the sailor suit! The least you could do is please your mother and eat some spinach. What will your friends think?"

"Think of you or me?"

"Curtis, if you want to run this spinach ranch you must learn to love it and sacrifice for it. Pride is something you must humble."

"I want to be a professional bowler."

"A what?"

"A professional bowler."

Vera approved of Curtis's choice when Sam disagreed, and Sam was the only one who wore the Popeye suit. Feeling alone, he got the brainy liberal idea of adopting the pickers as his children. He would order Popeye sailor suits for all of them and they would pick his spinach, wearing the famous suit. Vera thought the idea would be an overhead expense and was completely unnecessary. Curtis left for the university as soon as the idea congealed in his father's brain. This left Alicia to whom Sam turned for approval because he also thought she was intelligent. When he asked her what she thought of the pickers wearing Popeye sailor suits, she opened her mouth in amazement, but didn't contradict or approve. She allowed Sam to run his idea through, which in itself ended up to be an approval heard by Sam's mind. Sam approved and that was what Sam wanted to hear because he was liberal with his thoughts. Besides, what other rancher was giving away free suits and all the spinach you could eat?

-16-

¡No Somos Conejos!

Spinach-picking day had arrived and Sam was ready to greet those who had picked oranges and strawberries and were now ready to pick spinach. Sam was bubbling with excitement as he welcomed the pickers with a speech that was a repeat performance of last year. The speech was, of course, in Spanish, and this was greatly appreciated, the applause rising above the fields. Yet the applause expressed a sour note of discontent. Sam, however, the kind soul he tried to be, was deaf to the note that didn't harmonize with his and proceeded to tell them that his ranch was run along liberal Democratic lines. The people were all ears but confused, as they had been for years. They hadn't come to vote for a president or dethrone a king. They had come to pick spinach. The wages were the same as last year's, but they could eat all the spinach they wanted.

Proud of the fact that he was feeding at least half of the world, Sam gave out several bags of spinach to let them taste of the food they would harvest. The men grumbled but the women took the bags and told the men to behave. The men, however, couldn't help themselves because they were men, and one man rose to his feet and said, "¡No somos conejos!"

(We're not rabbits!) Everyone laughed, and Sam was taken aback by the statement he had misheard as, "¡No somos *cojones!*" which translated loosely meant that these men were impotent or something of the sort and that eating spinach would make them into rabbits.

"¡No somos conejos!" the old man repeated for Sam's sake and proceeded to eat several spinach leaves that had been handed out to show Sam what it meant to be a rabbit!

"¡No somos conejos!" several men began chanting.

Sam, who had looked forward to smiles and thanks because of his giving nature, looked at Alicia for help. She had stood silently in her Popeye suit so as not to rob him of his spotlight. Seeing such a good man, who was trying his best to educate the world about such a healthy plant as spinach, being eaten alive by these ungrateful men, she stepped up and said, "You are nothing but rabbits! You don't understand what this man is trying to do for you!"

"Eh, it's the bologna girl. And she's wearing a sailor suit just like him."

"Do you think maybe she found that millionaire man?"

"They look married to me."

"You complain all the time, especially the men. When you have nothing you complain, and you complain when people give to you."

"Have you eaten spinach!?"

"Shut up and let her talk!" the women cried out.

"Yes, I have eaten spinach. And it has made me strong," she yelled like a champion about to flex her biceps to prove to the men that women, too, could be as strong as men if they ate spinach. Of course, being the proper woman she was, Alicia didn't flex her muscles in public.

"I have eaten spinach in many dishes. And the señor here will give you recipes, which I have prepared myself."

The women applauded Alicia, for they had never heard a woman speak so decisively about spinach and recipes. Then Sam told them that there would be a surprise after several reels of Popeye cartoons, which he felt would boost morale and productivity if they thought like Popeye. Before showing the cartoons he had been bred on, Sam insisted on them chanting, "Popeye! Popeye! Popeye!" At first only Sam could be heard chanting. Then an old man took up the chant and pretty soon everyone was crying the sailor's name out just to get the cartoons over with. Of course, once the cartoons started rolling on the large outdoor screen, the men and children enjoyed them as they laughed at the skinny sailor getting beat up by the fat hairy sailor who eventually got beat up by the skinny sailor after he ate his can of spinach. They especially laughed when the skinny woman with long legs got stretched out and almost split in half. That was funny! Once the cartoons were over, there was that rumbling of discontent as they clamored for more Popeye cartoons. Of course they were hungry for more, and Sam, an avid fan of his hero, showed cartoons until they were fed up with the reruns. Alicia was amazed by the magic of cartoons on grown men as she watched them eat spinach as the skinny sailor did. Many of the children, seeing how strong Popeye was, ate themselves silly on spinach as if it were popcorn. Pretty soon, however, they would all be running into the fields with diarrhea.

After the cartoons were over, the men flexed their muscles, and all of them thought they were Popeye thinking the others Bluto, and a massive fight ensued as old wounds were reopened. Jimenez's wife was thrown out as an insult. Pedro's sister was made pregnant again. José was jerked out of his truck, killing himself again. The battle, however, didn't last long as Sam blew his whistle and the men stopped their imagination short of killing the cartoon Bluto they saw before them. The women got a last kick in as they hit their husbands over the head for believing they were men instead of rabbits.

Sam, however, applauded the battle that just taken place, and in another speech, in Spanish, he praised the men for thinking like Popeye. Someone mentioned tequila, but Sam was quick in responding that Popeye was a decent man who never drank.

"So what kind of sailor was he if he didn't drink?" someone dissented.

"A man isn't a man if he doesn't drink!"

"That's right. A man has real *conejos (rabbits)* if he is a *cojone (testicle)*."

"You are smashed, old man."

"A real man has *cojones (testicles)!*"

"No, a real *conejo (rabbit)* has *cojones (testicles)!*"

"You are stupid!"

Sam blew his whistle again and told them that at the end of spinach-picking time, he would throw a fiesta with all the spinach they could eat and all the tequila they wanted! And frijoles and tortillas and cerveza! They applauded the tequila part and were ready to go to sleep when Sam yelled, "Don't go yet. The fun's just beginning."

"Is the spinach-picking time over?"

"In your dreams, Manuel. We haven't even started."

"Maybe if we ate it all, we wouldn't have to pick it, eh!?"

"You must want to be a conejo for sure. I can see those ears of yours growing from your thinking of spinach."

Alicia, seeing there might be another fight, yelled that there were presents. The women, hearing that, told the men to shut up. Silence quickly rose out of the chaos, and all eyes were glued ahead of them. Sam brought out some boxes and like a magician, hoping to please his audience, pulled out several sets of sailor suits and handed them out by sizing people up as either small or medium. The women were especially eager to open their packages and as soon as they ripped through the plastic, ran into the fields and returned squeezed into sailor suits. Bellies, buttocks and breasts hung out of pants and shirts too small, but the women didn't complain even if the men laughed at them.

"What did you ever give me, Pepe?"

"What did you ever buy me, Juan?"

"And that man, a complete stranger, bought us a suit!"

"He is a man!"

"Sam is a man!"

"Sam is a man!"

"Sam is a man!"

The women chanted the slogan for a while along with Alicia, who thought the world of Sam for helping her people out. The men, as to be expected, didn't chant anything, although a few of them, those who had liked the cartoons, silently approved of Sam without applauding him. Some were antagonistic and walked away, leaving their plastic packages unopened. In the morning, Sam was truly disappointed when he saw only the women wearing sailor suits while the men remained men in their own clothing.

Before the women dispersed, Alicia handed out packs of recipes, and the women were surprised by the cards. Alicia explained how to make spinach into many dishes. She was so proud of her own newly acquired culinary abilities that she got carried away and mentioned the quiches, soufflés, and ratatouille she had learned to cook. The faces on the women were puzzled by the sudden linguistic change. What was Alicia saying? What was a soufflé? Alicia told them to read the cards. The women shook their heads. When Alicia's enthusiasm subsided, she realized that her own mother had not been able to read and that some of the women or maybe all of them couldn't read either. Shamed by her own pride and knowledge,

Alicia ran after the women and promised to come in the evenings and to teach them how to read and cook the spinach into fantastic hors d'oeuvres and pièces de résistance.

"You talk funny, bologna girl!"

"What is ordure?"

"I will teach you later."

Then out of the blue, a young girl cried out that the cards were not in English but in some strange alien language perhaps spoken by the people who lived on the moon. The women wondered what language the recipes were in before they would start teaching their own children how to cook and read. Alicia mentioned that the recipes were in French and that they had nothing to worry about.

"By the time we learn French we will starve to death!"

"I heard French is like Chinese!"

"You are so stupid, Juanita. It is almost like our own language."

"If it was like ours I would be able to read it."

"Of course you would if you could read your own."

"Don't get so smart with me, Laura. Just because you can read don't make you a spinach cook like that bologna girl!"

"At least she made something of herself."

"What? A stupid sailor girl?"

"Maybe she found herself a millionaire husband?"

"Maybe if we eat spinach we'll find millionaires too!"

Alicia promised she would return and teach them the recipes she had at first not understood.

The following day was not like any other day even though Alicia remained in the house, cleaned and cooked. She prepared her lessons, ready to teach her sisters how to become as good as the French cooks in Paris or New York. Her day seemed slow as she watched the men and women picking spinach. The women were wearing their newly acquired suits. The men had decided not to look like their wives or they too would become women. Alicia looked at their bodies moving like turtles over the green fields, and she suddenly felt alone in a world where she did not belong. Yet she didn't feel that she belonged out there anymore either. As she sensed this sudden alienation, she wondered if she would have the courage to re-cross the river and go home again.

Alicia had eaten many spinach dishes. Yet her taste buds were like wild roses yearning to be tickled by the feet of bumble bees. She wanted to taste homemade frijoles and tortillas. That night she fed Sam and Vera the usual soufflé and went out to see if Pale Moon and Yellow Rose had come.

Yellow Rose greeted her as a mother would her long lost daughter and invited her to eat some frijoles and tortillas. Pale Moon greeted her with her pregnant belly. She couldn't remember if the child was the product of the hamburger she had eaten or the young Mexican boy she had allowed to enter her so that he could lose his virginity. Yellow Rose didn't seem bothered by it at all. Running Antelope had threatened to kill the boy when he found out his name. Yellow Rose was glad Alicia had found her place in the world, although she couldn't see why she was wearing that stupid suit. Pale Moon and Yellow Rose had sold their suits for a few bags of frijoles. All the Indian women refused to wear the sailor suits. They also refused to eat grass that would turn the Mexicans into rabbits.

"Alicia, we cannot eat what is not ours! We eat our own food. They will certainly grow rabbit ears. Your ears have grown since we saw each other last."

"What?"

Pale Moon laughed as she saw Alicia searching for a mirror. Yellow Rose handed her a piece of broken mirror and Alicia pushed her ears to see if they would retract, but they didn't. The more she looked at them the longer they appeared.

"I like the spinach, Yellow Rose."

"I see."

"Pale Moon, do my ears really look longer? Tell me the truth."

"My mother's just fooling with you. Don't believe everything old women tell you. I met an old witch in the desert once and she told me you could get pregnant just by pricking your finger on a cactus needle. What did she think I was? The old witch still thinks young women should believe in the old ways. Do I have to believe in something stupid?"

"Yellow Rose. . . . "

"He has been by, and he has asked about you, Alicia."

"I didn't come to ask about him."

"He still loves you. He is still a boy inside, Alicia. To tell you the truth, he is still a virgin, but this is between us women. He should remain a man with the illusion of having made love to a woman. He just doesn't know how to express his love, Alicia."

"I want a man to tell me he loves me and prove it with deeds."

"If we lived a hundred years ago he could have died for you in battle."

"I don't want a dead husband."

"What do you want?"

"I don't know! A man who can carry me across the desert and fight off the enemy that would attack us."

"Alicia, take off that sailor suit before you turn into a cartoon!"

"Mama, I think she looks good in it, and I like her short hair. I'd give anything to live in that house with her and the millionaire!"

"Then Pale Moon, you should go with Alicia."

"But I don't really like it there. I feel very alone. I would rather be out here."

"Then Alicia, you must be stupid! I would like a house like that!"

"Shut up, Pale Moon," Yellow Rose said.

"When will Running Antelope come again?"

"He'll find you when he's ready. He is really full of passion for you."

"Tell him I love him too."

"You tell him."

"A woman doesn't tell a man she loves him, Yellow Rose."

"Then neither of you will know what love is."

That night Alicia had a dream, and in it she saw Running Antelope standing in the desert with the sun to his back. As she came closer she noticed he was naked, and she, who had never seen a grown man naked before, felt warm under her flesh. In this dream, she could not see herself. As a matter fact, she had never been able to see herself in any dream. So she didn't know if she too was naked, and she was quite happy to know that she was wearing clothes when Running Antelope spoke to her.

"Why are you wearing that sailor suit, Alicia?"

"I have to wear something. Why are you naked?"

"We are in the desert. Does it matter if I am naked? And why are you blushing?"

"Because you are indecent."

"I think it is indecent to be wearing that suit. Take it off, Alicia, and free yourself from the spinach man. Can't you see what Popeye has done to you?"

"You don't understand, Running Antelope. I was hungry after you left me so abruptly, and I didn't want to work in the strawberry fields. So I came here, and they made me feel like one of them. These are good people."

"You have eaten from their hands too long, Alicia, and you now think you are a woman because you are wearing a Popeye suit. The spinach has gone to your head."

"I am a woman, and I am as strong and as intelligent as you. I learned how to cook quiches and soufflés!"

"And you pronounce French beautifully. You are strong and intelligent, but think now! Do you need that sailor suit to make you strong? You are a woman with or without the suit."

"You just want to see me naked. No man has seen me naked."

"All I want is for you to be free of the Popeye suit."

When she awoke in the morning, Alicia was smiling, although she couldn't remember if she had taken the suit off or not. She had, however, heard Running Antelope clearly, and instead of putting on the suit, she put on a dress she had bought with her own money. When she came down to fix Vera and Sam's usual spinach omelet, Sam's mouth dropped and exclaimed his disappointment. Alicia broke the eggshells and whipped up the yolks and whites, her eyes staring at the old-fashioned skillet while Vera read the papers aloud and reran the story with her name in it to make sure all in the room remembered that she was performing a great duty for society. Not being blind to the goings-on around her, she praised Alicia for standing up for her own rights as a woman.

"You wouldn't catch me dead in that Popeye costume," Vera said, smiling as she left the room to lock up more rapists and murderers behind bars.

Sam appeared devastated by Alicia's move to wear her own clothes. He had made her into a French cuisinière and a member of the Popeye team. Alicia noticed his disappointed looks and his untouched spinach omelet, and she suddenly felt guilty. Sam looked like a poor puppy with tears in his eyes, but Alicia tried not to show her reaction. Then he had to open his mouth and express his thoughts and feelings and he said, "I gave to you out of the kindness of my heart, Alicia. And all I wanted was for you to wear the Popeye suit with pride. Is that too much to ask?"

"You know, señor, I am very grateful for everything you have done for me. I really liked the French lessons, and the cooking lessons too. You taught me that spinach can go a long way, but I don't want to wear this suit."

"It's just a suit, and it would make me happy."

"Your wife doesn't wear it!"

"Vera never liked Popeye, and she resents my calling her Olive Oyl. She taught Curtis to hate him too. I am all alone, Alicia."

"I am sorry you are feeling bad, señor."

"You can still call me Sam."

"Okay, Sam. Just because you gave to me, for which I am grateful, you cannot ask me to wear that suit!"

"It's okay."

"If you want me to leave, I will go."

"Oh, no, Alicia, what made you think such a thought? Stay, stay and maybe you'll see that the suit is harmless and that wearing it will make you think more positively."

"I need to go now to teach the women how to fix quiche with spinach."

"Please, pretty please, wear the suit. It will make you look professional."

"I think my people would prefer I wear this dress. Is it okay if I take eggs and cream this evening?"

"Take anything you want. You know we don't begrudge you anything."

"I know, señor!"

-17-
¡Huelga! ¡Huelga! ¡Huelga!

Alicia could not eat breakfast anymore because the food belonged to Sam and Vera, and she didn't want to fuel her guilt with any of their spinach. Sam insisted that she eat her spinach omelet, but Alicia told him she would rather get paid real money from now on and that she would rather work in the fields with the rest of the women. Sam was distraught, hearing such radical thoughts expressed by a young woman he himself had taught. There was nothing worse than a pupil rebelling against the teacher. How could she take so many steps backwards and allow her education to go to waste? Alicia took the eggs, butter, flour, cream, and other ingredients, along with the French cookbook she now despised for creating such a chasm in her life.

The women were given the day off with pay (all the spinach they could eat) if they were willing to improve their lives by cooking spinach dishes from French recipes. When Alicia arrived with her basket of ingredients and cookbook, she had lost the enthusiasm she had felt a day ago. The women were all eyes waiting to see Alicia in action. Not one to disappoint those who expected so much from her, Alicia proceeded to make the crust for the quiches, which she baked for fifteen minutes and then mixed the eggs, onions, cream, and spinach and poured it all into shells and baked them.

As they waited for the quiches to bake in the portable oven, some of the women expressed their complaints.

"Alicia, it is very nice of you to try to teach us new things, but we can't eat these recipe cards, you know!"

"Nobody is asking you to eat these cards. It is only information for you."

"She doesn't understand."

"It isn't that hard to make this quiche. You saw me do it. All it takes is eggs, butter, cream."

"Stop, Alicia. We might as well eat the recipe cards."

"You'll see how good the quiches I have made for you taste."

"Alicia, you haven't worked in the fields long. You have always lived with the bosses. We can't eat what you eat because we can't afford eggs and butter. If we have enough gas money to get us to the store then we have no money left for food, and if we have money for food then we have no money for gas!"

"Besides, we hate spinach!"

"My José hates it. It gives him diarrhea."

"We're not rabbits, Alicia. Tell the ranchero we want money, not spinach."

"Why should he listen to me?"

"Because he likes you."

"That's when I was wearing the sailor suit."

"Wear it for us, please!"

"I can't."

Alicia lost all appetite to teach. She collected her cards that were in disgusting French and marched towards the house like a passionate martyr ready to walk into the fires of Hell to save the innocents from sure death. When she walked into the house that had sheltered her from the outside, not realizing that she too had belonged out there, Sam was putting some cartoons together to amuse the men and children so that they would grow up strong like Popeye and learn to love spinach. Alicia, who had been passive and malleable in Sam's hands, continued to march ahead into the guest room, walked up to the television set and like a mother concerned with her children's mental well-being, shut the cartoons off. Sam was flabbergasted by Alicia's actions. After all, this was his house, and she wasn't even a guest. But being the polite man he was, he didn't curse or damn her. Instead, he smiled, and the smile incensed Alicia even more.

Alicia stood in front of him like a shield, her breasts thrust forward ready to receive the fatal bullet in the heart. Before she lost control of her thoughts she threw the recipe cards on the coffee table. Sam picked them up and his face seemed sad all of a sudden. He had taken time to print them out so that the "native" women learned something about civilization. Alicia then lectured him on her own stupidity. She had been so busy thinking of her own belly and well-being that she had forgotten that many of her people couldn't even read their own language. What good were cards in French to them? What good were the cards? What good were the recipes even if they were given orally when they couldn't afford a dozen eggs? What good was the spinach?

The last phrase offended Sam very much, and his true nature burst out of the suit that had molded his character for so many years that he thought everyone lived in his world. He defended the spinach he grew, the spinach that fed the poor of the world, the spinach that had created Popeye, the spinach that had made him into Popeye. After restoring his hero to his pedestal, Sam remained polite. Alicia looked at his face, and the smile she had at first misunderstood as kindness turned into a mouth with bloody lips. She was frightened by the vision she had just seen, but she stood daringly against him

and without losing her temper she declared that she could not
remain under the roof that stifled her soul. She would cook a
few more meals for him and Vera until they found another
girl, and she would even train her. She belonged out in the
fields with her people. She was yearning to taste frijoles and
tortillas but restrained herself from putting down Sam's sacred
spinach. Sam, of course, was sorry she was feeling this way, but
he couldn't force her to do things that were against her will.
She would get the same wage as everyone and all the spinach
she could eat. Alicia walked out of the house that had at first
attracted her, and as she walked along the fields, she suddenly
felt heavy chains fall from her legs. She felt so free that she
couldn't recall any of the quiche or soufflé recipes, and whatever French vocabulary she had shoved into her brain vanished
like a snake trying to fight off its own extinction.

When Alicia returned to sleep and eat with her own people, the young women, especially Pale Moon, looked at her as
if she had lost her mind. They called her "la loca bologna girl"
for not seeing that a nice house was better than the open sky.
Now she would have to eat frijoles as they did. They wondered
why Alicia would give up a clean bathroom to shit with them
in the fields. They were dying to know what a soft bed and a
shower felt like. They wanted to be able to open a refrigerator
door and pour themselves a glass of orange juice. Some of the
women had opened refrigerator doors at the appliance store to
get the feel of it all, but they were disappointed by the vast
emptiness in them.

Why had Alicia given up the life of a queen? The question
was on the tips of their tongues. Many thought she was crazy
and different from them even if she was back in their camp.
Those who had wanted to change places with her thought she
was a traitor when she had lived in the big white house and

was a traitor now for being back. Even though she was back they still thought that she thought she was better than them, and they wished she had stayed in the white house.

The men thought Alicia had done the right thing by coming over to their side. They also thought she had gone out of her mind, but there must have been a reason for it. Women thought the world was crazy because it was so, but the men thought the world was crazy because of reasons. They sat over tequila and discussed, like professionals, the reasons why Alicia had gone loca.

"It's the air in that house, I tell you. When I entered through the door, I suddenly felt like my breath was taken away. It was so white and light in there I thought I had died and . . . "

"And gone to Heaven! Aha ha ha, Pepe! Every time you go inside one of those houses you think you go to Heaven."

"I think Alicia was brainwashed like I saw done in a movie once. Did you hear how funny she was talking? I am glad our women didn't wanna cook. It's those quiches and soufflés that made her crazy."

"It's the spinach!"

"I agree. It's the spinach!"

"I don't eat it."

"Me neither."

"But the women do!"

"That's right. And Alicia did too."

"I noticed how my wife is too tired to make love to me."

"Maybe she's got another man."

"Why should she look for another man, José?"

"Maybe she likes a man with bigger cojones?"

"Leave his cojones alone, Emiliano. We are talking about our women. Why do you always bring up such filthy words when we talk about our women? We are decent men, and we need to figure out what spinach can do to us. My wife had a dream, and in it she had turned into a frog, and then through some kind of magic she turned into a princess. And ever since she's had the dream she keeps wanting all sorts of appliances: toasters, refrigerators, televisions, and cars. And I asked her where we put all this stuff, and do you know what she tells me, 'Buy me a mansion like that one!'"

"And my wife wants diamonds and a stupid gold watch!"

"And mine a mink coat. I tell her we live here in Texas."

"What do you need a mink coat for?' She says, 'I get cold at night.'"

"Aha ha ha! That's funny, José. You see you really don't have any cojones because if you did, she wouldn't be cold and need a mink coat to keep her warm."

"Emiliano, will you leave his cojones alone! I hear your wife wants not just a mink coat but a polar bear coat!"

"My wife doesn't eat spinach!"

"Let's not fight like dogs!"

"We must do something because our own children are no longer listening to us. My boy wants a racing car he saw in a magazine."

"Mine just wants a burro!"

"At least he can feed the burro spinach and grass all he wants here."

"We must do something!"

"We must talk to Running Antelope."

No sooner had Running Antelope's name been mentioned than the air was filled with hope for salvation. That night Running Antelope was back in their camp like a warrior ready to wage battle. He stood above them near the campfire, his hands creating a world not in Heaven but a negation of it. He had learned from Karl that theories were good on paper but that they didn't feed the people's bellies. And that men had to be reminded they were men. And that Emiliano had the right to have his own cojones and not someone else's. And that men who ate spinach were not strong like Popeye. Men were not rabbits! All the men who had eaten spinach leaves had gotten diarrhea and forgotten their own names, but also forgot who their wives were and almost strayed with the first woman they saw.

Spinach was the devil's weed! Spinach was a sinful weed! It made men impotent but lustful! It made women pregnant with goats. It made women dream of other men and refrigerators full of food. Spinach caused women to want abortions. Spinach made their children little thieves and disobedient sons! Spinach made their daughters want to marry men with Popeye suits!

Running Antelope was filled with fervor and gave them the energy to raise themselves on their own two feet even though they were tired from having picked spinach for Sam Popeye. Running Antelope had heard of the cartoons the ranchero had shown them and pointed his finger at the white mansion and told the men to behave like men and not children or all of their minds would be erased by the Popeye character, and they would never be able to remember their names. It was time to put an end to his tyranny. The people made themselves known and began to shout, "¡Huelga! ¡Huelga! ¡Huelga!"

Alicia had not yet learned of Running Antelope's return, but in her heart she felt that he would soon make his appearance. Meanwhile she continued to serve Sam and Vera their special dishes and even though she refused to live in their house, they were polite to her. As a matter of fact, Vera was all smiles now that she had moved out and that she no longer wore the Popeye suit.

The night the strike was being organized, Alicia was preparing dinner for Sam and Vera and the minister of the First Baptist Church and his wife. Although Sam and Vera considered themselves Methodists, they spoke to people of other faiths, which made them very liberal. Alicia noticed that the meal wouldn't just consist of spinach soufflé, spinach salad and spinach jello. There was roasted lamb! The lamb of God was being roasted to please the Baptist minister's palate and his spouse's predilection for sheep. The minister and his wife were apparently almost complete anti-vegetarians and ninety percent carnivores, and Sam and Vera made it known that they respected men and women of every walk of life. Alicia was impressed, but nonetheless disturbed by their lack of sensitivity to her people.

Alicia served the meal but was not asked to join them at the table this time. She suddenly realized that she was out of place as they began eating. The minister, whom Alicia remembered for his sermons on the lustful and sinful behavior of man, was smacking his lips loudly. Although his face was young and pleasant, Alicia couldn't help but imagine a pig's face instead of the human head that was stuffing its mouth with the lamb of God which she thought belonged to her people. The minister's wife ate small bites and seemed ashamed of the meat she was eating because Sam and Vera were only taking food that was made with spinach. Her mouth was small, and she didn't speak because her husband was doing all the talking.

"My wife's pregnant again as you can see. It's our fifth child to be born through the grace of God," the minister said to fill the void. Sam and Vera said nothing. His wife said nothing. Alicia couldn't understand why they had been invited if no one was really talking. The knives and spoons did most of the talking. Of course, the minister had to speak or he would go mad because of the silence.

"The world has become an awful one, Sam. Sinful! Every time you pick up the papers or turn on the TV all you ever see is murder, rape, theft! Especially among wetbacks! There's no teaching them folks civilized ways, is there? I must tell you, this lamb is delicious. We Baptists follow in God's footsteps, and we do eat lamb. We do not eat pork, however! Back to what I was saying. These people are heathens and must be converted to our ways. They must learn that sin is what leads to committin' crimes!"

"Our workers do not commit crimes," Sam exclaimed, while Vera patted his hand and added, "Mr. Flate is not talking about our pickers, dear!"

"Oh, yes, I am, Ma'am! Pickers are pickers, and they do pick fruit. And didn't Eve pick the first fruit!?"

"We grow spinach here," Sam said.

The minister's wife had stopped eating and was looking pale, perhaps because of her pregnant state.

"We don't have problems here, Mr. Flate," Sam was saying in a loud voice.

"Well, I'm glad to hear it, Sam, but in time you'll find out that wetbacks will eat you out of house and refrigerator."

"We give them all the spinach they can eat!"

"While our own people starve to death?"

"I'm not starving the American people! Do you know, Mr. Flate, that our own people wouldn't pick spinach for a living?"

"Please, let's not argue so violently! We are, after all, civilized human beings!" Vera interjected.

"Please, honey, can we go? I'm not feeling well," the pale minister's wife asked timidly.

As the minister was about to take up where he had left off, Alicia exploded and said in perfect Americanese, "I have seen you fuck prostitutes!"

A heavy silence shattered their argument, their faces shocked by Alicia's obscene statement. Once they recovered their composure, Sam apologized for Alicia's lack of knowledge of the English language while Vera smiled uncomfortably. The minister's face was red with anger while his wife's had grown one shade paler.

"I don't have to listen to this kind of talk! I am a man of God!"

"A man who screws putas! You screwed my sister!"

"Alicia, you don't know what you're saying," Sam cried out.

"We don't know where she picked up such slang," Vera said apologetically.

"If you wanna know what I do there, I'll tell you. I go as Christ did into the darkest areas of town to save these women's souls from damnation. But you, young lady, can only see the sordid side of life! Kindness to you means nothing!"

"So how come you gave my sister fifty dollars?"

"Because she's poor!"

"You screwed her as you did Running Antelope's sister."

"This woman's insane!"

"And my sister had gonorrhea!"

"My God, that's why I can't pee!" the minister's wife cried out of the blue as the minister grabbed hold of her hand and said, "Your maid is making things up as she goes along. All you wanna do is drag a good man down. All you wetbacks are alike. Let's get out of this spinach maniac's house, honey! I'll see you burn in Hell, Al—whatever your name is!"

"Why can't I pee, honey?"

"Let's not get personal until we get home."

"Why can't I pee!?"

"You're pregnant, that's why! Let's don't make a scene like you always do!"

As they opened the door to leave, the minister and his wife were greeted by men and women with signs and torches yelling, "¡Huelga! ¡Huelga! ¡Huelga!" with Running Antelope at the head. Sam's and Vera's mouths dropped to the ground, their eyes filled with fear and disbelief. Alicia smiled as she looked at her people awakening from the dream that had kept them imprisoned for years. The signs varied and made their point. Pepe waved, "¡No somos conejos!" next to Victor who carried a message for all mankind, "Man cannot live by spinach alone! A little lamb would help!" His message was too long and could hardly be read. "Christ never ate spinach!" "Spinach causes pregnancies!" "Spinach causes abortions!" "Spinach is for gringos!" "Spinach for rabbits!"

Sam stepped up politely and waved his hands to calm the sea of people before him. Alicia left the porch and stood next to Running Antelope. Sam spoke.

"You're all fired! Get off my land!"

Alicia was surprised to hear such harsh words come from a man she had considered gentle and kind. Running Antelope jumped up on the back of pickup truck and said, "You can fire us, but there will be others who will come and they will be organized. I will organize them, Mr. Popeye! Meanwhile nobody'll pick another leaf of this spinach!"

"Get off my land!"

"We were too kind to you, Alicia! Is this the way you repay us?" Vera yelled across the commotion.

Sam and Vera closed the door to the crowd of puzzled faces that now surrounded Antelope to find out if their demands for lamb and wages would be met. Had their signs had any effect on Popeye? They had not understood his words and demanded a translation that would not betray them. When Alicia told them they were all fired, their voices rose against Running Antelope and his progressive ideas. Alicia could see anger in their burning eyes and quickly led Running Antelope away before they pelted him with rocks and hanged him out to dry like a skin off a deer's back.

-18-

Words Are Worth Their Weight in Gold

Instead of hearing words of love come from Running Antelope, Alicia nurtured his ego all night. He wondered what he had done wrong this time. Alicia told him that there was no way of predicting what men like Popeye might do. A man with a steady smile was as dangerous as a rattlesnake with sharp fangs. Mr. Sam Popeye could always hire pickers whenever he wanted to, and they would be happy to eat all the spinach they wanted and they would not complain for a while until their bellies were full and their mouths got bored with the tasteless spinach weed. Hunger will make men do funny things. They will humble themselves, become rabbits even. Then when they are full they will turn into wolves in rabbit clothing. The new pickers would have to be very hungry, she told Running Antelope.

Only in the morning did Running Antelope ask Alicia how she had fared away from him. Hearing such concern, she was glad he had a heart and soul after all. For a while she had thought that all men could only think about themselves. Alicia told him that she was ready to go back home and to learn to live there instead of dreaming. He agreed that perhaps it would be better. Then out of the blue he exclaimed that he might give up his crusade and join her across the river. He had always wanted to try his hand at gardening, and he might be able to teach the people in her village to grow real fruits and vegetables.

Running Antelope was off on another idea, and no sooner had he dug the garden, planted the seeds and picked the fruit of his thoughts, than he was ready to teach the people what they would need to survive. Alicia listened to his plans and joined him in the garden he was creating and ate of the fruit with him. She was happy to be by his side.

"We must learn to grow our own food, Alicia, because soon there won't be enough to go around. These gringos will have money and machines, but no food. You can't eat money or a television set. And you sure can't eat what they show on TV. I will teach your people how to grow things."

"Running Antelope, I don't think we should teach anyone anything. Let us dig our own garden and grow our own vegetables."

"What about the people?"

"They can't be taught yet. They eat the food they dream of."

"Why is it they don't die?"

"We have lived on dreams and hope for centuries. And even when we are dead our people are still hungry and still hope. The spirit always yearns."

"I understand."

In the morning they parted with Yellow Rose and Pale Moon and took the road south. The pickers had returned to the spinach fields after sending an apology to Mr. Sam Popeye, who kept his promise and let them eat all the spinach they wanted.

As they began their walk on the asphalt road that boiled like a blue ocean with mirages of cars and cactus, a radio announcer's voice exclaimed that Mr. Ira Flate, minister of the First Baptist Church, had been brutally murdered in an alley. The news didn't reach Running Antelope or Alicia because they had no radio and even if they had had one the news wouldn't have concerned them. But no sooner had the news hit the airwaves than a police car zipped down the highway in search of none other than Alicia and Running Antelope.

The police car stopped them and a tall lanky officer with a sympathetic face pulled his gun on them and told them they were under arrest for the murder of Mr. Ira Flate. Running Antelope told the officer he had never heard of the man. The officer promised he would hear much more about him later. Alicia couldn't understand what that pig's murder had to do with her until she reached the police station where she was read her rights. An investigator asked her if she had ever made any threats against the dead man. She shook her head. The investigator made a face and read her a statement written by Sam Popeye and Mrs. Vera Popeye, who claimed she had verbally threatened the dead man's life. The officers shrugged their shoulders and one of them said that Mr. Popeye's words were worth their weight in gold around here. The other officer, with the sympathetic face, said he couldn't believe what she was saying because she was from across the river. He had apparently been dealing with her kind for years, and her kind was known for exaggerating the facts.

"Lyin's more like it!" the other exclaimed as he separated Alicia from Running Antelope. She cried out his name like an animal wounded in the desert. He told her not to worry. And Alicia believed him because he knew the laws of this country. After all, he had been to Yale law school and graduated with honors.

Alicia was taken to a cell where several women were locked up. A raspy voice in the dark yelled, "Fresh meat's coming!" and someone laughed. Although frightened, Alicia didn't want to show her fear. The police officer unlocked the door and without warning shoved her into the cell as if she were an animal. Alicia fell on her knees and cried out in pain. The raspy voice now stood above her. Alicia got up as quickly as she could before the voice pushed her down for reasons unknown. Alicia saw that the voice belonged to one of the many lizard women lingering in the dark. The raspy voice with make-up that made her look like a piñata asked her if she had murdered someone. Everyone laughed. Alicia wondered why that was funny and found a spot for herself in a corner of the floor and tried to close her eyes to erase the nasty scene that had invaded her sight. Perhaps when she opened her eyes, the lizard women would be gone.

Alicia suddenly realized that Rosa might be there amongst the lizard women and like a mother, she got up to search for her lost child. "Have you seen Rosa?" she asked politely. The lizard women were not moved by her polite question. Many of them blew smoke in her face. Some spit in it. Others growled like mangy dogs not wanting to be disturbed. Alicia couldn't understand why there was not one compassionate face among them. She had thought that perhaps among her own people, among women who had been downtrodden and abused, she might find one face who would speak to her like a human being.

Alicia sat back down, her heart suddenly hard and empty against these women who felt nothing. As she began to entertain harsh thoughts against them, a voice as gentle as a nightingale's addressed her by name. Alicia turned in the direction the words had come from, but could see no one. She peered through the dark, but still no one was there. She thought at first that Rosa was playing tricks on her. With the make-up and the dark, Alicia might have missed her face. She called out Rosa's name and cursed her for being cruel. The lizard women told her to shut up and rolled over to sleep.

Alicia remained silent, waiting for the voice to reappear, but no one wanted to speak to her. She closed her eyes, and no sooner had she done so than an old woman in rags appeared seated next to her, her face as wrinkled as dry clay, eyes burning like two blue marbles filled with hope and life. Her hands were wrinkled also and covered with scales, which caused Alicia to withdraw as they touched her.

"Alicia!"

"How do you know my name? I don't know you!"

"Don't be frightened. I have known your name since you were born, but I did not live to see you grow. I come from the same village you live in. I was born there and I died there. I knew your grandmother quite well. She is busy right now cooking tamales for the angels."

"Angels eat tamales?"

"You would be surprised what angels eat, Alicia. They eat frijoles, tortillas, but they don't eat meat!"

"Do angels get married?"

"There's no need to get married. There are enough angels to populate a thousand Heavens. But I'm not here to talk about angels, Alicia."

"Why are you here?"

"You must be careful. A man will come to see you to defend your honor. He will be kind, gentle, and handsome. He is not a millionaire, but he will fall in love with you when he sets his eyes on you. Do go with him even if you do not love him. We women up in Heaven have watched you and we want what's best for you. He is very handsome, Alicia. The Indian that was with you will rot in jail and lead you to poverty. He will get you pregnant and you will hate your children and your husband. You will hate the desert flowers, the river, and the rain. And you will hate yourself. Go with the man who will defend your honor and forget the Indian. We women saw him fry on a chair. There is no sense in grieving for the dead man even if he is alive, Alicia."

"But I love him."

"Alicia, you cannot love someone in a dream. You will wake up and he will vanish like the morning dew!"

"But I don't love the man who will come to defend me."

"You can learn to quickly, Alicia. He has a very nice house, a beautiful patio with flowers that give off such aromas that you will forget you were ever born. He has several cars and three refrigerators full of food. He owns fields covered with strawberries and cotton. You will never go hungry in his hands. He speaks like a poet with a golden mouth. Alicia, you must forget the Indian."

"But he is innocent. He was with me the night of the murder."

"You must either be crazy or as stubborn as your grandmother. We women thought you came across the river to marry a millionaire, and now you are defending a pauper. No woman in her right mind would do that. Besides, Alicia, the police and the judge will believe that you were with him, but they will not believe that he was with you."

"That doesn't make sense. He was with me, therefore I was with him."

"He's an Indian, and no one believes Indians because they are Indians."

"But Running Antelope doesn't lie. He is a man of honor."

"Running Antelope must be a liar because he is an Indian. That's a belief no one will change."

"But it doesn't make sense."

"Neither do you, Alicia. You must go with the man who will come to defend you or you will fry with the Indian. This would hurt our hearts very much, and what will I tell your grandmother?"

The old woman stopped talking. Her hands became scalier than they had been. Her eyes seemed to burn bluer and as she rose into the air, Alicia noticed she had a lizard tail. She disappeared into a cloud, and Alicia opened her eyes to the morning light piercing through the window above her. The lizard women were coughing and grumbling. The raspy voice declared that she was starving. Someone let out a big gush of gas, but no one noticed it except Alicia, whose memory of the old woman with scaly hands was quickly fading.

Alicia tried to remain still, to recall words that now were vague in her mind. One of the lizard women lit a cigarette and the moist air suddenly became acrid and smelly. She crawled to an empty corner, raised her skirt without shame and defecated into a pile where roaches and flies were congregating for breakfast. Alicia stared at the pile of feces and was revolted by it. She imagined Yellow Rose and Pale Moon, her own mother, Rosa, and all the people she had met crawling to the top of the pile, but every time one of them reached the summit, an obese spider pushed them back down. The people would roll down, their faces covered with brown slime and sweat. They caught their breaths and up they went even though the obese spider stood in their way.

One of the men on the pile cried out that they should kill the obese beast, and then they would be able to rule themselves and eat the fruit of their own labor. The man made a spear and he quickly mounted the hill carefully behind the spider. He lanced the spear into the spider's chest and blood covered the man. With a loud moan the spider died and rolled downhill where the people beat the beast with sticks and stones and cried out with joy that they were free at last. They all rushed up the hill, but the man who had killed the spider had suddenly turned into the obese spider himself. The blood that had sprayed him had apparently caused the transformation. The obese spider, not remembering that he had once been a man crawling up the pile, hissed and growled at those who were climbing up the hill to kill it. Several spears went through its chest and blood gushed out like a dam suddenly breaking under heavy rains. The drops covered the faces and bodies of the men and women, and they too sprouted eight legs and furry black bodies. Once they had been transformed into obese spiders they began fighting among themselves trying to make it to the top.

The lizard woman, noticing Alicia's stare, pulled her skirt up. "You like what you see, honey?" she asked as she walked up to Alicia and let out a gush of gas right in her face.

Alicia said nothing as she rose to her feet, waiting at the bars for someone to get her out of what she thought was a bad dream. She blinked her eyes several times to make the lizard women go away, but the scene at the pile did not vanish as others defecated on top of the people-spiders climbing to the top of new piles where roaches waited in competition. Alicia would have wept for herself, but the tears she felt would not come out of her eyes because of the anger and fright she had against these people who were not of her kind even if they spoke her own language. But even their words were different from hers. They flicked their tongues out like frogs and spat obscene words she had never used. They were coarse and harsh. They were cruel. They wounded her.

The sun was rising outside, and the rays awoke the other lizard women. They began to stir, smoke rising from their red lips. They did not disturb her anymore and she was very glad. Their stomachs seemed to grumble in unison, obscenities boiling in their hungry bowels. They began yelling for the guards to come and feed them breakfast. No one came for a while, and the lizard women grew impatient. Finally the officer with the sympathetic face emerged from the darkness. In his hands he was holding a muffin with eggs and ham. He took a bite out of it and said, "Your breakfast will come when you ladies learn to behave yourselves." As soon as he said these words, he left the hall with curses and spit covering his beetle-like back, and the lizard women got louder because they knew the men would get tired of their screaming and would feed them to keep them quiet.

Out of the chaos created by the lizard women came a cook with a cart covered with plastic containers and the food that would fuel the lizard women to keep them alive and to enable them to multiply their own kind. An officer accompanied the cook and with his nightstick hit several hands away from the bars. Before opening the door, the officer told the women to kneel and to recite a prayer he had been taught as a boy. The lizard women all knelt immediately as if to obey his wishes. Alicia remained standing and didn't see why she should have to kneel to an empty prayer. The officer's face remained sympathetic and smiling as he tried to stare her down to her knees. As the officer opened his mouth to praise God for the food the lizard women were about to receive, Alicia opened her mouth and openly defied the officer for his mockery. She unleashed her anger against the lizard women who were more concerned about their bellies than they were with truth. The officer was offended by Alicia for denying him his right to pray for the food these women were about to receive, and he told her to shut up. The lizard women all called her a stupid puta, and Alicia felt lost under their accusations and the officer rejoiced as the lizard women repeated his favorite prayer. He served them breakfast with his own two hands to show them that he was a true Christian capable of obtaining repentance from others. When it came to Alicia the officer turned a blind eye and erased her from existence. She wasn't hungry anyway.

Alicia Maravilla

While the lizard women were eating their food, licking their lips and fingers like ants trying to get the last morsel, Alicia tried not to smell the aromas that mingled with the foul odor in the corner of the cell. As she thought of the outside world, the river she wanted to cross again, the cactus flowers, the raspy voice touched her shoulder and said, "You got guts! We were just playing with you yesterday to see what you were made of. You passed the test. Here's half of my muffin. You're gonna need it."

At first Alicia was wary of the food so freely given. Would the raspy voice bite her hand as she took the piece of muffin? Alicia reached for the muffin, and the voice let it go into her palm, and Alicia thanked her.

"We're not evil, you know," the raspy voice said and moved back to her kind. Alicia was about to take a bite out of the egg and ham muffin when the officer with the sympathetic face rushed in and called out Alicia's name. Seeing the muffin in her hand, his face filled with wrath. He slapped her wrist and the muffin flew out.

"You don't get to eat unless you thank the Lord for the food you receive from His bounties!" he screamed for all the lizard women to hear. Then he looked around and counted the muffins that were still being eaten. When he came to the raspy voice, he demanded to know where her muffin was. With defiant eyes, the raspy voice said, "I gave it to her because she's more of a person than you'll ever be!"

The sympathetic officer opened the door and told Alicia to come with him. When he closed the door, he threatened the raspy voice with disciplinary action and then led Alicia out of the darkness into the light.

-19-
Can Love be Bought?

Alicia was led into the light and left in a room alone. Before she could ask herself why she had been taken here, a man of average size, wearing a blue suit and carrying a brown briefcase, walked in. He introduced himself as José Hernandez, attorney at law. His face was youthful. His eyes, playful and brown, seemed to search for something absent from the room. His pencil-thin moustache made him look like a mouse, which disgusted Alicia. He asked her to sit down and relax. After all, she wasn't being taken to the electric chair yet. Hearing such a thought, Alicia's soul shook with fright.

The man before her insisted that she call him José and to trust him, only him, because the world, as she must have realized by now, was one crooked place. He would save her from a possible death sentence, which he kept bringing up, if she told him exactly what happened the night of the murder. Alicia thought she would go free once she explained that she and Running Antelope talked the whole night through. José the Lawyer took her hand and with reassurance in his voice said, "I believe you."

"I am so glad someone believes me, Señor Hernandez."

"Call me José. Now I think you will be able to go since you have an alibi."

"What's an alibi?"

"It's an excuse for not being guilty."

"It's not an excuse. It's the truth. I was with Running Antelope all night."

"I believe you were with him all night, and Mr. Sam Popeye is willing to believe that too."

"I knew he was a good man."

"Yes, he is good and forgiving too."

"Can I go now?"

"Yes, but it's not so easy."

"Why? What about Running Antelope?"

"He is being held for murder."

"Murder? He was with me all night."

"That's what he keeps telling me, Alicia, but he hasn't convinced me of it yet. Something in his voice tells me he killed Mr. Flate. Do you know what it means to kill a minister in this part of the country? To kill a man of God is like stealing a herd of horses. The man could be hanged and put to the electric chair after that."

"How can you kill a man more than once? That's cruel."

"Man dies many times, Alicia."

"He was with me."

"No, you were with him, but he was not with you. You must think about yourself. I hate to do this to you, but if you continue to claim that Running Antelope was with you, you will go to jail, and if they don't execute you, you will grow old and wrinkled, and maybe someone will kill you while in prison. Your life will be wasted. Alicia, you are a beautiful woman. Such beauty ought not to be wasted. Now, was Running Antelope with you? Think hard, very hard."

"No," she answered with resolve.

"Good. That is good to hear! You are free to go with me. You will be under my custody until the trial."

"What trial?"

"Running Antelope's, of course. You must testify that he was not with you."

"Of course," she said.

José the Lawyer opened the door and led Alicia to the outside world. His steps were quick and jerky as he spoke of the wonderful state of affairs. Alicia half listened to his stories that dealt with various crimes, which were good for business. The world wasn't as bad as everyone thought, at least not for him. He preferred murders to rape or divorce, but he only represented those who could pay for his services. A murderer who couldn't pay for his services deserved the chair because he was poor and therefore guilty since birth. Thieves surely deserved to go to prison. If they had money they wouldn't be stealing. If they stole they had no money, and if they had no money they couldn't afford his services. Murder was his specialty. It was interesting and it gave him a sense of being. It allowed him to live through the passions he seemed to lack in his own life.

As they drove to his house, José kept his mouth running. He was a man of many words that had to fill the air and the woman he was trying to impress. He was not married and had one child somewhere across the border that he had forgotten once he reached this bank of the river. Alicia wanted to know what had happened to Running Antelope. When his name touched her lips, her heart almost melted as she felt it fill with blood. It fluttered with palpitations. She was in love. Hearing such a question, José the Lawyer stopped the car alongside the highway and began yelling angrily. His face suddenly turned into an ugly sight that resembled a dog's with foam dripping from its rabid mouth. He banged his head against the steering wheel as if trying to smash his skull. Then he turned to Alicia, his forehead bleeding and cried out, "Don't ever mention his name again. He is as good as dead! And you must forget him for your and my sake. Do you see this blood flowing from my head? I bleed for you. This blood is the blood of my love, Alicia."

"But you don't know me. How could you love me?"

"I love you because I am willing to die for you! I fell in love the day I heard Sam Popeye utter your name. There could only be one woman with such a name in this world. Alicia! Alicia! I repeated your name until it became my prayer. And you answered it. If you want to have a life with me, you must forget the Indian. He is nothing but a troublemaker. Some build. Others destroy, and he is only willing to destroy what others have built. Forget him, Alicia."

"I can't."

José the Lawyer never thought of Running Antelope as he showed Alicia the life she would lead with him as his wife. He took her around the mansion he had built like a Spanish hacienda with its centrally located fountain and patio with flowers and cactus. Here she would be able to cultivate roses to her heart's content. He had dreamed of a woman growing roses for him for years, and now that she had appeared, like a goddess, he was certain that she would love to cultivate roses because he had recently purchased all the books ever written on raising roses. Alicia touched one of the petals, and this was a good sign to José the Lawyer, who knew she would be a natural with flowers until Alicia pricked her finger. The drop of blood on the tip of her finger brought a sudden tear to his left eye. Only one tear, but it was so large that Alicia felt sorry for him. She wiped his tear away, and the smile of self-satisfaction rose from his lips like a plume on a volcano. His smile made her afraid of the thoughts he might have been entertaining.

Alicia told him she was allergic to flowers, especially roses. The lie didn't please José the Lawyer, but he had other trinkets up his sleeve.

He took her through the mansion and pointed out the wall-like television set that had thirty-nine channels. He showed her the pool table and the many games she was welcome to play anytime. He opened the refrigerator, and his mouth ejected words: melon, orange, yogurt, lamb, crab, shrimp, lobster, pate, roast beef and red wine. The last two items caused her stomach to quiver as they brought back lessons she had learned. The roast beef and wine had been part of a dream when the dream was innocent and not real. But what was to prevent her from tasting of the dream itself and remaining who she was? Would she forget Running Antelope just because she would eat some roast beef and drink a glass of red wine? She had heard of men forgetting their own names once they had eaten a certain wild weed, but what could roast beef and red wine do?

Alicia stood frozen in front of the refrigerator like an aborigine struck by the whiteness of men come to annihilate him. Her stomach was empty and in pain to be filled with food. Her heart was torn between her love for Running Antelope and her survival. José the Lawyer understood her longing stare and pulled out the plate of roast beef. He led a semi-conscious Alicia to the lace tablecloth and sat her down. He took a long carving knife and slowly sliced a fresh succulent piece of meat that smelled more of flesh than meat with a scent of garlic and pepper that made her nostrils quiver with delight and her mouth water with the forbidding taste of a dream come true. The slice lay on her plate, medium rare. Unable to resist its alluring look, she began eating the meat. José the Lawyer was delighted. He rejoiced like a child suddenly happy because he has taught his puppy to roll over. He poured her a glass of wine and Alicia, who had not had anything to drink for almost two days, drank several glasses, which made her drunk and dizzy, but she was still aware of her surroundings.

José the Lawyer wanted Alicia to be full and pleasantly plump like his mother. He thought Alicia was too thin, but under his guidance she would grow into the image he had in mind. He hated the thin look American women were so fond of. He thought plump women were more loving and caring, like his mother had been. He brought out more roast beef, microwaved some potatoes, stuffed her with salad, pudding and then ice cream. Unable to control herself, Alicia ate everything in sight only to throw up a sea of red wine, roast beef and other particles. This did not make José the Lawyer happy. His food had not delighted Alicia's palate, and this pained his heart. Alicia lay down on the couch and José the Lawyer covered her with a blanket. She closed her eyes and fell into a deep sleep.

A familiar river flowed through a valley where orange groves lined only one shore and not the other. Men with dogs and guns walked up and down the orange shore, while men, women and children with hardly any belongings waited for nightfall on the other side. A young man, who looked like José Hernandez, was walking across the river in broad daylight. One of the men with guns waved his rifle telling him to go back, but José Hernandez yelled back in Spanish, "What are you going to do, shoot me?" The man's face grew angry and without giving another warning, shot José Hernandez in the belly. He fell under water, but then rose out of the water as José Hernandez, the lawyer. He was walking dressed in his blue suit and carrying his briefcase towards the shore where the man with the gun stood waiting for the boy he had shot to float downriver. José Hernandez stepped up to him and said, "Here's my card. If the boy ever wakes up from the river, tell him to find me. I am his lawyer and judge."

Then José Hernandez became a boy again, and he was back in a village that too looked familiar. There was a porch with a young girl whose face was covered with sweat and tears. She would wipe her tears, but every time José Hernandez, the boy, would open his mouth, her eyes would swell up and explode with more tears. The young girl's belly looked big, and José Hernandez kept pointing to it and saying that it wasn't his. This made the young girl sad and angry. She defended her honor through her tears and after he was through accusing her of nasty deeds, she threw a flowerpot at him.

José Hernandez, the boy, was unmoved by the young girl's show of genuine emotions and walked away. Instead of following him and begging him to marry her, the young girl continued crying not for José Hernandez but for her favorite and only flower pot, whose pieces she was picking up one by one, perhaps hoping to glue them. Not hearing his name called out, José Hernandez, the boy, turned around, his face hard like stone and defiant. His eyes seemed to burn with great passion.

"I want to be free of this village! And you tie me down with this child! Maybe it's Father Romero's!" he yelled.

José Hernandez, the boy, vanished from the village dust. The young girl was sitting on the porch, but she was now holding a baby and singing a song to it. The baby was tugging at her breast and sucking on her nipple. "I will name you Alicia!" As she heard the young girl call out her name, it kept repeating itself until she opened her eyes and saw José Hernandez the Lawyer with his mouth close to hers.

Alicia, frightened by the closeness of his face and the foul smell from his mouth, pushed him away, yelling, "You are my father!"

"You are crazy!"

"I had a strange dream, and you were in it!"

"Just because I was in your dream doesn't make me your father."

"Dreams tell the truth! Did you leave a pregnant girl across the river?"

"Please, Alicia, listen to me!"

"You did!"

"It was a long time ago in another dream!"

"Dreams don't leave you, Señor Hernandez!"

"I don't believe you're my daughter, Alicia. You are mine, and I want to marry you."

"Don't touch me!"

José Hernandez the Lawyer rose to his feet like a man defeated but unwilling to give up Alicia's image.

The days wore on. José Hernandez the Lawyer would disappear dressed in his blue suit into the early morning light, leaving Alicia to herself. The first day she tried to walk out of his house, she found the doors locked and the windows barred. José Hernandez had warned her against thieves, which was a problem because people were innately bad. He also warned her against escaping. There was an elaborate security system and the bars at the windows were electrified. He wouldn't want to find her dead. Alicia felt like a bird in a gilded cage. The food José Hernandez fixed her didn't taste good. At first he thought she might be homesick for her native food, but even the frijoles and tamales remained untouched. Alicia looked at the food but did not touch it. Then José Hernandez remembered the roast beef and red wine she had found tasty to her palate, even though she had gotten sick. He placed a fresh piece of red beef in a pan, covered it with spices and chunks of garlic.

The aroma from the meat and garlic filled the air and like spirits unleashed, it invaded her nostrils, lungs, and stomach until she herself became the roast beef she had so often dreamt of. When José Hernandez the Lawyer set the table, carved the meat and poured the wine, Alicia noticed that his face was that of a lizard. Was she hallucinating because she had not eaten a

S. Leconte

single bite of food for days? The roast beef made her hungry and sick at the same time. He invited her to the table, but she didn't respond to his invitation. He proceeded to eat by himself. She would rather starve than give in to a man she didn't love and who might be her father.

José Hernandez the Lawyer observed that she was getting pale although he knew she must have been eating while he was out of the house. Yet when he counted the fruit and made written observations of the cheese, bread and meat, he noticed that Alicia had not touched a single morsel of his food.

Alicia knew that she would die if she didn't eat, but she would rather be dead than eat this man's food. Death to her and her people meant that this dream would end and another life would begin. The food was part of the dream that too would end. Its aroma was just a bad spirit trying to take possession of her mind and soul.

José Hernandez the Lawyer did not relent, and like a man bent on securing the image in his dreams, he persisted with the food he thought would bring her back to her senses. Alicia kept her mouth and nostrils shut, trying not to breathe the spirits she thought would possess her. She began to think that José Hernandez the Lawyer did not exist, but he wouldn't go away, and his voice kept bouncing around the room like a vulture, offering her food stolen from the gods that lived up near the mouth of the volcano near her village.

Alicia seemed asleep when awake with José Hernandez there to tell her that she was still among the living. She was tired and weak, but he knew she would eat out of his hand one day. As she got weaker, he realized that this was no ordinary woman he was dealing with. She could not be bought with food.

Since food was not an item that could convert her soul to his way of thinking, José Hernandez the Lawyer decided there were other ways of catching a woman. One day he showed her

221

several large boxes. Alicia didn't even wonder what he was up to. Like a bird trying to impress its mate now that the nest was prepared, he opened the boxes and smiled at Alicia as he placed the ring in her hand. Not being able to respond emotionally, she dropped the large piece of glass she didn't know was a diamond. His face seemed disappointed, but he placed the ring on her finger and declared her his fiancée. Then he pulled out a white wedding gown and stood with it as if he were prepared to wear it. She had seen such a dress in a magazine and knew it was a wedding dress. He placed the dress on her and told her she would become his bride. Time would erase all bad memories that she might be harboring against him. She would even grow to love him because he was José Hernandez the Lawyer, whom the world respected for his honor and integrity.

One day while he was at work, Alicia heard on the radio that Running Antelope was going to trial, and her heart and mind, both of which had not forgotten his existence, almost failed her because of the shock. Each day after that, she turned the radio and television on, hoping to catch a glimpse of his being. Then one day she decided to eat bites of food to give her body the strength it had been losing. The bites were inconsequential and went unnoticed by José Hernandez the Lawyer. As she grew stronger, she continued to lie around like an actress playing the part of a woman dying because of man's crime against women. She regained her strength within a few weeks. The trial meanwhile had just ended and the jury was deliberating Running Antelope's guilt.

The jury returned the verdict within a half hour, which was the longest a verdict in this region had ever been deliberated, especially since it dealt with an Indian, who was guilty until proven innocent, a view that had become law since men believed in their own goodness as José Hernandez did. Running Antelope was found guilty of murder in the first

degree and sentenced on the spot to avoid wasting the taxpay-
ers' money. Alicia was shocked to hear such news when she
knew he had not committed the awful and brutal murder.

The night of the news José Hernandez the Lawyer
returned home with a face glowing with hope. Alicia knew he
was happy Running Antelope would soon die on the electric
chair, and she hated him for thinking evil of the man she loved
ever since she had been deprived of his presence. In her mind's
eye she saw José Hernandez the Lawyer's hands choking
Running Antelope until there was no life in him, and she
hated him even more. Yet she didn't allow her anger to show
as she lay on the floor, her face unable to look at the man
behind her, for fear of giving her feelings away. While they
were preparing to murder Running Antelope, José Hernandez
the Lawyer spoke of his deep love for her, and how she needed to eat some food to be able to stand by his side in front of
the priest who would marry them once the bad dream with
Running Antelope was over.

José Hernandez the Lawyer's mood was reaching the high
point in his life. He seemed to be one big wire of energy ready
to electrify the world with his happiness, while Alicia prayed
as she had never prayed in her life for Running Antelope to do
something.

-20-
A Dream Come True

After Alicia recovered her strength, she came to her senses and declared she would have to marry José Hernandez if she was ever to feel the sun on her face again. If she married him, she would at least be able to walk out of the house. When she had heard that Running Antelope's appeal had been denied by the higher courts, her heart almost broke, but there was nothing she could do for him, and he nothing for her. If only she could have testified, then perhaps the jury would have believed that there was no way he could have murdered the minister because he had been with her all night, and she had been with him. But this was not logical on this side of the river.

When she announced her decision to marry him, José Hernandez lost his composure and mind. Unable to believe his ears, he lost all power of speech, went blind for a minute or two, and his heart began racing a mile a second. The shock of the news could have caused him to die of a heart attack. Men have been known to die of such a state from news of a lesser magnitude. José Hernandez was hearing the music of the sirens that sailors hear at sea, and he thought he was dying and going to Heaven. He lay down to recompose himself.

While he was in this weakened state, Alicia could have left this prison and walked to the river and crossed it, never to return again. She could have stolen his keys, wallet, money, plastic cards and charged José Hernandez' life to the devil, but she didn't. Instead, she rushed into the kitchen and wet a dish-cloth and applied a cold compress to her future husband's forehead. No sooner had she touched his head than he opened his eyes and said, "I am feeling all right, Alicia!"

She was amazed by the speedy recovery that love brought about. At least that's what she thought until he opened his mouth and came out with a truth that hurt her deeply.

"I am feeling fine."

"But I thought you were dying."

"I don't die so easily, Alicia. My father is still alive and so is my grandfather. My great-grandfather died at a hundred and thirty-five. And if it hadn't been for the rattlesnake that bit him, he would have lived to be two hundred!"

Hearing such news concerning his longevity, Alicia suddenly had second thoughts. How could she live with a man who might live to be not one hundred but two hundred years old?

"I'm all right. I was just testing your loyalty to see if you would have left me to die and to see if you would have walked out. I am glad you care for me, Alicia."

When she heard that he had tried to trick her, Alicia, like an almost married woman whose love has been doubted, flew into a rage that made José Hernandez into a happy man convinced of Alicia's love for him. He was especially convinced of her deep feelings for him when she slapped him several times and then scratched him on the left cheek, almost taking out his left eye. The pain and the blood made José Hernandez into the happiest man in this world. What other woman on earth could have shown him so much affection? As she continued to hit him, José Hernandez' joy was diminished, and the pain suddenly became real and so painful that when she hit him in the right eye, he had to pull away from her.

"You make me so happy, Alicia, but please, try to control yourself. You can hit me tomorrow but for today give it a rest."

"I hate you!" she yelled.

"A woman who hits like you do cannot hate. It is your love that you are expressing."

"How could you doubt me? How could you not trust me? José Hernandez, you tried to trick my feelings, and I don't like it. If I ever have to experience this again, I will leave you to die!"

"Oh Alicia, you are so sweet when you are angry!"

Unable to contain his happiness, José Hernandez the Lawyer drove off after locking the doors. Her promise of marriage had not unlocked the doors to his heart, and he still did not trust her. He returned several hours later and unloaded boxes of presents. She spent hours opening them and expressing her deepest joy by oohing and aahing at the ring, necklace, toaster, dresses, brassieres without cups, panties, negligees, toys of various makes, several stuffed dolls, and much more.

The following day he surprised her when he was about to leave for work and said, "I will leave the door open for you today. You can go for a walk, but do not disappoint me."

"I will not, my future husband. I will be here when you return."

José Hernandez the Lawyer did not add any of the threats he might have. He could have said, "By the time you reach the river, I will have the police waiting to meet you there." But he said nothing of the sort. He simply walked out and then drove off without kissing her because she wasn't ready to be kissed by a man not yet her husband, especially when that man might be her father. That thought revolted her.

Once he left the driveway, Alicia resumed her normal breathing, relieved that he was out of her sight. She then listened to the news, trying to find out something about Running Antelope's fate, but he was already old news, and his being would not be resurrected on the radio or television screen until his day of execution. After scanning the airwaves for traces of her beloved, she decided to take a walk.

The outside air greeted her with the rising sun that was coming out of the desert east of where she was standing. And it was as if she were seeing the ball of orange rise for the first time in her life. She felt as if she too were rising into the clouds, but a car horn quickly brought her back to the ground below. The driver's face yelled something incomprehensible and drove away. She got back on the sidewalk. All of a sudden she had the feeling that someone was watching her. She looked around but saw nothing that might have aroused her suspicions. Surprised not to see José Hernandez the Lawyer's face behind the wheel of his car parked anywhere, she returned home.

Like a housewife out to please her husband, Alicia wanted to prove her undying love to secure his confidence and trust. She cooked him several dishes: a salad, a paella, a custard, and some homemade bread. She cut some roses and other flowers whose names she would never find out as long as she lived. She arranged the table like a maître d' about to execute his customers with a meal fit for a king. She was out to kill his doubts and cast them into the desert to burn. She was out to make a believer out of him. She changed into a black dress, and as she admired herself in the mirror, she wondered if she was really here in this house. Or was she merely a reflection of herself cast here for punishment?

When José Hernandez came home, his mouth dropped and his eyes burst into tears from the sudden revelation he came to. Alicia could have disappeared but hadn't. She could have pricked her fingers while cutting roses but hadn't. She had put on the black dress to drive his senses wild, but she told him to behave himself like a good boy if he didn't want a rerun of the beating he had gotten the night before.

José Hernandez was a man tasting of Heaven on earth. He was truly in paradise. His palate satisfied, he walked out on the patio to smoke a cigarillo, which Alicia lit for him to prove that she was to be the woman of his life. A man on fire from passions hard to extinguish, José Hernandez attempted to touch her several times in several places, but Alicia either pushed him away or slapped him.

"Get those nasty thoughts out of your head. I plan to remain a virgin until I get married."

"You are still a virgin?" he asked like a man surprised by the fact that someone could have a sense of respect for her own nature.

"You make it sound as if it is something to be ashamed of."

"No, you shouldn't be ashamed. I just thought that. . . ."

"I was a puta!"

"How can you think that I would think such a thing about my future wife?"

"Why do you try to undress me then? You must learn to respect me, José Hernandez, before you can have me. Even after I marry you I may not give myself to you."

"But you will be my wife then. If you love me as I love you, you must give yourself to me then."

"Just because you say you love me doesn't mean you can take me."

"Alicia! Alicia! Why do you complicate things?"

"You have complicated them, not me. You must learn respect before you can love. Are you willing to wait a year or maybe two after we are married before I make love to you?"

"Alicia? You are asking for a miracle."

"José, I am not joking!"

"Yes! Yes! I will do anything to have you by my side. I don't care! As long as you are by my side and men think I have the most beautiful woman in the world, nothing else matters. I will wait a hundred years to make love to you."

"I am glad to hear that, José! Good-night!"

"Good-night, Alicia my love. I will dream of you."

"And I of you."

In the morning José Hernandez the Lawyer would drive off, and Alicia would repeat her routine to please the man of the house to be. She varied her recipes and dresses and left José Hernandez more speechless each time, his fantasies heightened to the point that love was breaking his heart, but he contained and restrained himself for fear Alicia would change her mind about marrying him. After a week of sheer surprises, José Hernandez the Lawyer dropped his guard and was no longer amazed to find her at home. Even while trusting her, he could not be certain that she would be there when he came home. Alicia was aware of his feelings. She was even aware of the eyes that had followed her from across the street. Lucky for her she had not tried to escape.

Secure in his love and trust, José Hernandez dismissed the eyes that had spied on her and left for work. His amazement diminished when he came home.

One morning after he had left, Alicia heard on the radio that Running Antelope had escaped from the maximum-security prison along with several other convicts. Hearing this piece of news, she put on her own dress and walked out the back door, her heart beating as if it were a hundred galloping horses. At first she was at a loss. Then looking at the rising sun, she walked parallel to it in the direction of where she thought the river to be.

Alicia ran without thinking at first. Then she recalled that Running Antelope and she had decided that if anything should ever happen they would meet near the large oak that

grew north of the obese man's orange orchards. The thought
of crossing the river there frightened her. Suppose the obese
man and Kyle were there, shotguns in hand? They would surely shoot Running Antelope and spare her. Or maybe not!

Alicia hurried like a bride escaping from the gilded cage
towards freedom and the man she truly loved. Time was running its course. She had to reach Running Antelope before the
police. She had to cross the river before José Hernandez the
Lawyer came home and found his nest empty of the woman
he had trusted. She could not be brought back or he would
make her life as miserable as he could for the next two hundred years.

She ran off the road into the desert, thinking of the oak at
the river crossing. The cactus all looked alike, she thought,
and pretty soon she realized that she was lost like a person in
a blizzard. Disoriented by the sand and the sameness of rocks
and plants, she was about ready to cry, but held her tears back.
As she stumbled back to the road, she heard her name yelled
with such force that she kept running from the sound of it for
fear that it was José Hernandez the Lawyer and the police. Her
legs, however, quickly gave in, and she fell face down into the
sand.

When the voice became clear, she turned around and saw
Running Antelope kneeling next to her. She touched his face
to make sure it was not part of a mirage or dream. His hair had
been cut short, but this was no time to discuss his hair. He
picked her up and carried her to the red pickup truck waiting
on the road.

The driver, who might have been typical for a Texan, prevented Alicia and Running Antelope from expressing the feelings they had felt away from one another. Even if the mouth
of the driver had stopped praising the best, the biggest, the
greatest grapefruit, toilet, hat, building, river, country that

Texas had to offer, they still would not have talked about the love they had kept away from one another in front of a stranger who knew no limitations to silence.

The man talked about anything his mind had not thought out while they squeezed each other's hand. Their eyes spoke of the pain and joy that reunions bring. They disclosed the friendship and love that was to come. The radio played on. The driver drove his drivel into the ground ahead of him, not expecting a response from either of them. Like the ancient ferryman, he got them to the river crossing in the midmorning hours, just as the radio announced that Running Antelope had escaped from a maximum-security prison and was wanted for the first-degree murder of a Baptist minister. The driver smiled and reached for Running Antelope's hand and shook it as if he were meeting him for the first time in his life and said, "Couldn't ever stand no preachin' from Baptist bastards when I was a kid." Holding on to Running Antelope's hand, the driver stood with them on the highway. Alicia wondered when this man would finish his new tale of the Baptist minister he once whipped for torturing his sister with hell and damnation for wearing lipstick.

Running Antelope managed to free his hand from the vice-like grip of the driver who wished them both the best of luck after praising him for the murder that made Running Antelope a hero in his eyes. Alicia and Running Antelope ran towards the river away from the orange orchards. They looked back once to see if the red pickup was still on the road. It was, and the driver was still waving at them.

They reached a safe spot in the river where the flow was slow and the water shallow. They looked around like rabbits sticking their heads out of the bushes and decided that it was safe to cross.

Alicia stepped into the warm water, her feet soothed by the flow that restored life to her soul. She looked into Running

Antelope's eyes but instead of seeing the joy she had expected in them, she noticed sadness. His hand let go of hers in mid-stream and she seemed to float away from him.

"Running Antelope, don't you want to come with me?" she asked, her voice almost fading from her own ears.

"I do! But I can't cross here. Every time I take a step, something seems to push me back."

"Try to cross somewhere else. I will wait for you at the mission over that hill!"

"I will see you there!" he yelled so that she would hear him. When she reached the other shore, she turned around to see if he was there, but he had faded like an image badly fixed in solution. It was as if he had not existed at all. Yet there was a deep and empty feeling in her heart, and she was ready to cross the river to find him again. But suppose he had already run to another spot and crossed the river?

Alicia hurried to the mission, hoping she would see Running Antelope greet her with open arms. How long she had waited to kiss the lips of a man she loved with all her heart in spite of his shortcomings! Her breath was almost swallowed by the emptiness of the walls. The pit of her stomach was vacant, and her heart sank into disappointment.

Alicia waited at the entrance of the mission like a widow expecting the return of her husband, knowing but not believing that he was a ghost her mind wanted to come to life. She hoped and prayed. She made several promises to God, and when night fell and brought the cool air to bear on the hot desert sand, Alicia found the same corner she had slept in months ago, which seemed like years. A jackrabbit huddled in a corner across from her. She closed her eyes and dreamed of the lady in blue who was handing her another rose.

In the morning she opened her eyes, and to her surprise heard her mother's voice yelling at Rosario in the kitchen. Her nostrils filled with the aroma of frijoles and tortillas, and it was as if she had never left home. When her mother came to her bed and saw her conscious, she raised her hands to her mouth and kissed her daughter as if she had just been resurrected from the dead. Alicia wondered why her mother was making such a fuss and asked how she had gotten home. Her mother told her she had been found at the mission two days after she had left to go across the river.

"But I went across, Mamá, and I found it to be an awful place."

"Alicia, you never made it. You almost died in the desert, and if it hadn't been for the young man who brought you home, you might not be here with me."

Alicia couldn't believe her eyes when she looked at the door entrance and saw Running Antelope standing there holding a rose in his hand as if he had been a part of this picture all her life. She knew in her heart that she had crossed the river and given birth to her future husband out of a dream no one could deny now that he stood before her in flesh and blood.